THE BIG BOOK OF
IN-YOUR-FACE
GAY ETIQUETTE

THE BIG BOOK OF IN-YOUR-FACE GAY ETIQUETTE

BY

Daniel Curzon

Daniel Curzon

The Big Book of In-Your-Face Gay Etiquette

Front cover motive '*le chat noir*' (the black cat) borrowed from the poster, which was designed by Théophile Steinlen, originally used to advertise a tour by Salis' '*Théâtre d'ombres*' theatrical group in 1896 at his infamously popular cabaret-théâtre. '*Le chat noir*' was already associated with a certain provocative, animalistic, sexual intelligence at that point, and it soon became symbol of the baudy, irreverent humor and the provocative art created by the actors and artists of *Montmartre* (at that time a northern suburb of Paris) during that period. The adjective '*chatnoiresque*' (black-catty) was coined specifically for that purpose.

Published by l'Aleph – Sweden

www.l-aleph.com

ISBN 978-91-7637-576-1

l'Aleph is a Wisehouse Imprint.

© Wisehouse 2014 – Sweden

www.wisehouse-publishing.com

*Being a Compendium of the Best Advice About,
and the Most Worthy Codification of,
the Standards of Good Manners
and Agreeable Social
Behavior*

🕊 BLURBS ABOUT THIS BOOK

"I loved it, or would have if I had been alive when I read it!"

— the Duchess of Windsor

ೠೞ

"Great bathroom reading!"

— the Count of Monte Cristo

ೠೞ

"I found it most fascinating, as I appear several times in its pages!"

— Lady Hammer

ೠೞ

"Corking! Spot on concerning all things etiquettish."
— Lord Langley, XXI Viscount Hogg

ೠೞ

"I hid my gin in this f***ing book until the end!"

— Princess Margaret

 # CATS

~ the epitome of graciousness

If you truly want to be the very best, the chic-est, most gracious, and yet maintain that line between friendliness and over-familiarity, you had best model yourself on our feline friends.

1. Cats eat only what satisfies the body, never entrails or extremities, unless of course if they feel peckish at four A.M.

2. Cats can delight themselves with small pleasures for hours, a bauble, a bubble, or Tweety Bird.

3. Persian, Siamese, Burmese, alley – cats will dally with many, seriously date the few.

4. The name *you* call me by is NOT MY NAME. I named myself long, long ago.

5. You will do what I want, when I want it, and be grateful I don't scratch your eyes out.

6. A disdainful stare can keep many a dog in his place.

7. One does not work. Life is too short. Others will feed you, if it comes to that.

8. Naps are essential for maintenance of one's inner beauty, to say nothing of the outer.

9. Don't lose your hair. You may lose your room and board.

10. God is a cat.

HOW TO TELL IF YOU ARE HOMOSEXUAL OR HETEROSEXUAL

If you are in mixed company (meaning with non-gays), you may, upon occasion, forget who you are. However, to keep your social bearings, just follow this handy guide.

Just Say the First Thing that Comes into Your Head

1. Pierce

    Het   *Homo*
    Arrow   Mildred

2. Judy Garland

    Het   *Homo*
    nervous breakdown   rainbow

3. Closet

    Het   *Homo*
    old clothes   old lies

4. Open

    Het   *Homo*
    golf tournament   getting fired

5. Tearoom
   Het   *Homo*
   gypsy   arrested

6. Basket
   Het   *Homo*
   goodies   Goodies

7. Lite Beer
   Het   *Homo*
   sissy   low in calories

8. Month
   Het   *Homo*
   a division of the year   a long-lasting affair

9. Trick
   Het   *Homo*
   or treat   Hello, handsome!

10. Log Cabin Republicans
    Het   *Homo*
    What?   Why?

11. Transgender
    Het   *Homo*
    Huh?   Right on!

12. You may not be as witty as Oscar Wilde, but remember you can still be arrested!

A GOOD ADDRESS

Should you live in a gay ghetto? It is a question that only you yourself can answer. Make up your mind by considering the pros and cons.

PRO

1. They speak your language.

2. You can wear native costumes.

3. You're near a movie theater that shows Alice Faye musicals.

4. You have such a large selection to choose from — at least half a dozen in the world!

CON

1. You have a gay accent.

2. Punctuality is the virtue of princes, not of queens.

3. You get beaten up by other "minorities."

4. You're never home.

 # OLD CUSTOMS

~ *self-esteem*

— Using "She" for "He" – Gone Forever?

Much to be lamented nowadays is the loss of a charming old folkway of many gay gentlemen of former times. We speak of the use of "she" for "he" in such quaint expressions as the following: "Who does she think *she* is!?" Anyone with fondness for the past must sigh that modern gay gentlemen now choose to designate each other with male pronouns instead of female, thus robbing us of our very own special "language," truly part of the splendor of our gay heritage.

We can only regret the failure of the younger generation to carry on this tradition of cozy intimacy and brotherly esteem. If only the junior members of our clan could recall those endearing days of yesteryear – the gentle satire, the robust interchanges, the warm symbolism of homosexuals' rightful place in society. If only the younger members could once again enter into those convivial circles (so *intime*, cut off, as they were, from the outside world) and live again those cordial and genteel times!

Yet apparently that is not to be. For modern esti-mations of woman and woman's place in the world have absolutely *ruined* all that! Never again can a gay gentleman put another in "her" place by assigning the designations of the opposite (and once inferior) gender. Alas, all we are left with is a pitiful and coarse equality that prevents the "girls" of times gone by from delighting in their friendly (and always mutual) contempt.

 SOCIAL DISEASES

~ Dear Dan Letters

Here are some of the very many letters we have received about *You Know What* with my —

SUGGESTIONS FOR THE SOCIALLY IMPECCABLE

Question:
What is the major cause of herpes simplex?

Answer:
Puberty.

Question:
What is the major cause of non-specific urethritis?

Answer:
Uretha Franklin, sister of Aretha.

Question:
I have syphilis, amoebic dysentery, and hepatitis all at the same time. What should I do?

Answer:
Did you wash your hands before you wrote this letter?

Question:
I have gonorrhea of the throat. What do you recommend?

Answer:
A hand job.

Question:
What is the proper treatment for anal warts?

Answer:
Listerine and voodoo.

Question:
I have a bluish color to my menstrual blood and pustules on my tongue. What do you think I have?

Answer:
My sympathy.

Question:

I like rimming total strangers, but I keep getting parasites. I do not wish to take Flagyl, as I've heard it makes one depressed. What should I do?

Answer:

Move to a new location, or at least your tongue.

Question:

I have several womyn living in my house. We are a commune. Our problem is that I have a persistent fungus in my vagina. We would like to get rid of it, since it interferes with the joy of our Lesbian sex. What do you think causes this?

Answer:

Obviously you are too good a host.

Question:

I have a fever, nausea, and yellow eyeballs. What do you recommend?

Answer:

Celibacy.

Question:
My stool is grey and has been for some time. What do you suggest?

Answer:
Re-decorate.

Question:
What is the major cause of syphilis and gonorrhea?

Answer:
Sex. It is also the major cause of marriage.

Question:
For several months now whenever I have sex I have a yellowish discharge from my penis and a burning sensation when I urinate. What do you think I have?

Answer:
A lot of nerve.

Question:
My hair has fallen out, I have a stiffness in my joints, and I am impotent. Do you think I have tertiary syphilis?

Answer:
No, you are probably dead.

Question:
There is a cute Jehovah's Witness who keeps coming into my hallway. May I entertain him in my apartment?

Answer:
Yes, but by no means convert.

Question:
I am a straight man about to appear in a commercial where I have to pretend to almost touch another man in a 'homo-erotic' way. Should I throw up while doing it or just act really, really upset and nervous?

Answer:
I mean it in the nicest way: Fuck you.

 GAY HOLIDAYS

January 1
>New Year's Day
>(for new resolutions and new lovers)

January 6
>The Feast of the Three Queens
>(of special interest to the Drag Community)

February 2
>Candlemas Day
>(for those who prefer candles to dildoes)
>(also known as Groundhog Day, for those who
>prefer groundhogs)

February 14
>Valentine's Day
>(annual VD check-up day)

February 22
>George Washington's
>(and Bruce Vilanch's) birthday (Maybe)

February 28
>Ash Wednesday
>(gays give up ashes for Lent)

March 21

Vernal Equinox

(spring begins; new resolutions, new lovers)

April 1

April Fool's Day

(and Malcolm Boyd's First Communion)

April 12

Passover

(*all* rabbis march for gay rights)

May 1

May Day

(gay Communists unite to celebrate forced labor
by gays under Communist regimes)

Second Sunday in May

National Matriarchy Over the Patriarchy Day

(also Mother's Day)

May 30

Memorial Day

(to recall past lovers)

June 21

Summer Solstice

(Longest Day of the Year)

(also Raving Feminist Rhetoric Day)

Last Sunday in June

The San Francisco Lesbian-Gay-Bisexual-Transgender Parade.

(and Questioning) (and Had a Homosexual Experience Once and Did Not Repeat It and Had Half a Homosexual Experience Once)

(Did we forget anybody???!!!)

July 4

Independence Day

(gays throw fire crackers (and beat up) punks for a change)

July 14

Bastille Day

(S&M gays have themselves locked up in a tower)

August 14

V.D Day

(Victory over V.D.)

First Monday in September

Labor Day

(also known as Unemployment Day)

Fall Blur

> The Folsom Street Fair
>
> (celebrate full-frontal whatever, be photographed by Asian tourists)
>
> The Castro Street Fair
>
> (walk around a lot, buy a trinket, be photographed by Asian tourists)

September 21ish

> Autumnal Equinox
>
> (fall begins; new resolutions and new lovers)

First Monday in October

> (celebrate the U.S. Supreme Court ruling overturning sodomy laws)
>
> *(Cheer . . . and now turn over!)*

October 31 / Halloween

> (with its tradition of punks coming to the Castro and starting fights, being homophobic up close)
>
> (being photographed by Asian tourists)

November 11

> Veterans' Day
>
> (gay and lesbian veterans celebrate dishonorable discharges. Don't ask. Don't tell. *Scream*! (in fond memory))

Last Thursday in November

Thanksgiving Day

(celebrate the crumbs we've gotten)

December 21ish

Winter Solstice

(. . . Hell, why not! New resolutions and new
lovers)

December 25

Christmas Day

(peace on earth, good will to men. *Where* exactly
is this?)

December 31

New Year's Eve

(feel sorry for yourself because you haven't got a
lover)

(Watch *All About Eve* again. Rejoice!)

 # ORGIES

~ must the polite host offer seconds?

1. Emily Post has little to say on the subject of orgies. Nevertheless, we believe she would approve of Kleenex as more sanitary than is a common towel and less pretentious than cloth napkins. (One may wish to share one's body with the multitude – but not one's best linen.)

2. Lube is preferred as a lubricant by nine out of ten orgiasts. Crisco was preferred by Julia Child. (Lard is used only by the lower classes.)

3. Fingerbowls are nice for tidying up after those occasions when digits *will* wander.

4. A small turnout need not dampen your orgy. If you are resourceful, even two can make a festive occasion. (One person at an orgy, however, tends to hamper creativity.)

5. Picking one's nose is frowned upon even in the most flamboyant orgy, unless of course all parties agree.

6. A mouthwash should never be gargled within hearing distance of other participants. To do so is to mark you as wanting in tact.

7. Spitting out in a post-AIDS world, on the other hand, is fashionable.

8. The proper music for an orgy is not Doris Day albums.

9. Orgies and friendships rarely mix.

10. Orgies and brunch never mix.

11. One may not yawn during an orgy.

12. Sending invitations with time limits (such as ORGY AT PHIL'S: 8-10 P.M.) marks one as a touch bourgeois.

13. Former Attorney General John Ashcroft may attend your orgy. But don't expect him to participate.

SPORTS

In spite of a different image, homosexuals are often interested in (and good at) sports – not to mention always being good ones. We know of numerous gay persons who have excelled at everything from rugby to tennis to baseball. Of course each may have a favorite, but the one sport that is almost universally popular is masturbation. It is even mentioned in the Holy Bible.

From youth onward, it is remarkably easy to grasp the rules and is never exhausting, unless one rises to truly world-class status. Most people are content to aim much lower. Professional masturbation is not always easily mastered, but if one applies him – or herself – a person can become adept and lose that amateur taint.

This sport has the advantage of being one of the few non-competitive sports, can be played by one or more players, and can be enjoyed even by the deaf, the mute, and the terminally ugly.

Although you may never wish to try out for the Masturbation Olympics, there are certain regulations that even the most uncommitted dalliers ought to be familiar with.

Consequently listed below are —

THE RULES OF POLITE MASTURBATION

GENTLEMEN'S RULES:

1. At least one mallet is necessary; two or more preferred.

2. Mutual of Omaha does not refer to a tournament of onanists in Nebraska, nor does this company insure players.

3. Coming on time is essential.

4. Fans are welcome to watch, but they must not shout or hiss.

5. Do not hold the mallet in your hand until it is your turn to shoot.

6. Resin is not recommended for sweaty palms.

7. Hitting another player's ball with your own is technically against the rules, but it is sometimes winked at.

8. Playing with family members is illegal but known to happen in Red states.

9. Solid strokes are more effective than half-hearted ones.

10. You will not go blind, unless you get so excited you poke yourself in the eye.

11. Goal: A sound mind in a sound body.

LADIES' RULES:

(Note: Ladies usually have more endurance in this sport than gentlemen.)

1. Ladies must use different equipment from gentlemen.

2. A playing field is necessary: a rubyfruit jungle, no time limit

3. Pushing and shoving on the playing field allowed, indeed encouraged.

4. Dildoes are allowed but don't tell the politically correct.

🦋 PETS

People of Gayness occasionally do not have children, and so they may want a pet instead. In the absence of any clear-cut rules, let us merely lay before you certain advantages and disadvantages of owning either a pet or children —

ADVANTAGES AND DISADVANTAGES

1. Obviously no human being ever "owns" a pet. *Quelle horreur!* (The pet owns the human being.)

2. If you have a dog, you don't need to spend money on Pampers (whereas children seldom have fleas).

3. It is easier to toilet-train a child than a monkey (or at least some children).

4. Monkeys seldom need braces.

5. Cats, unlike children, never need nightlights, bring home bad report cards, or sniff glue. (But cats also rarely do the dishes.)

6. Birds infrequently track in dirt, tell fibs, or beg for fudgsicles. (They also seldom smile.)

7. Dogs lick your hands and are grateful for almost everything (whereas kids seldom chew the furniture). Both, however, occasionally run away from home.

8. Gerbils are not argumentative.

9. Rabbits never suffer from constipation.

10. Children grow up and leave you. (Pets stick around but die.)

11. Pets never ask you to baby-sit the grand-children.

12. Children sometimes forget themselves. Elephants remember your birthday.

13. Horses let you get on their backs (whereas children want you to get off theirs).

14. But then again, children tend to wipe with toilet tissue.

— No one can make the decision for you.

CLOTHES FOR THE CRUISE

~ what is low and vulgar and what is smart

Do clothes make the man?

Well, it depends on the kind of man you want to make.

Still, no matter who you come into contact with, you will be judged by your appearance. Therefore, you must take pains to dress well.

Besides, human frailties being what they are, very few of us are seen to greatest advantage when totally naked.

In addition, the garment industry would suffer enormous hardship, probably triggering a worldwide depression, if we didn't wear clothes. So we are protecting the economy by dressing well, and often.

And, if we don't dress up, our already over-crowded hospitals will be filled with clothing fetishists suffering from nervous breakdowns.

So, if anyone accuses you of overdressing, you can remind that individual of these enumerable virtues and know that you are in the right and he, she, or it is probably, at best, a latent nudist!

Now undoubtedly one of the most important times for dressing is when you are going out to cruise. On those occasions you cannot be too careful about how you look.

Please pay heed to the following **Suggestions**, which we have set down with great precision after long experience in the field —

Next to you skin (which must be bathed, scented, and talced) you should put the briefest of underwear that you can find. No self-respecting gay man wears long-johns, even in Minnesota (Lesbians may differ here, as in other matters.) Only *boxers* wear boxer shorts. The unliberated wear Fruit of the Loom, and panty-hose are for panty-waists. If you wear something truly chic, you wear something that holds up your genitalia and thrusts them forward to edify and intimidate, as it were, all you encounter. Some people go without underwear completely so that they are indeed ready for any action that may pass their way, but then again they risk disfiguring hernias. Dirty underwear is never suitable for wearing, only for sniffing.

Next you don a shirt which shows off your finer points, such as your well-exercised pectorals (but which hide your love handles). Name brands are important, so if you can make people realize you are wearing a designer creation, by all means advertise this fact by letting the label show, or possibly leaving a price tag on. (While it was once thought insufferably vulgar to do such things, nowadays it is the height of *haute couture*.) (Must we add that Walmart is not a designer label?)

Definitely keep at least the two top buttons of your shirt unbuttoned, to reveal your chest hair, which you have tinted if grey or plucked if such exceed three dozen per square inch. (Back and shoulder hair, need we mention, is unspeakable, and the less said about it the better.)

Ties are worn only by businessmen in the office or by Radclyffe Hall.

T-shirts may be substituted for real shirts if you are a member of an Olympic team, or wish to give that impression. If you feel compelled to have words on your T-shirt, make sure they are clever or discreet, like "Wanna Fuck?" T-shirts with messages are most appropriate in dim room or on deaf-mutes. At least spell words correctly!

Next you must put on a pair of tight pants, preferably of a solid color. If you choose stripes or patterns, be sure that you are slender, under the age of seven, or over the age of eighty. Trousers with the buttocks cut out are considered cheap, even in California.

Placing a salami down your trouser leg is considered smart in some circles, for when you are dancing or just moving about you will want others to notice that you are well-hung. On those evenings when you wear such an appendage you clearly *may not* go home with anyone, because your partner's disappointment when you undress might cause him to faint or turn your over to the Fair Trade and Practices Commission for false advertising.

A handkerchief may be placed in a rear pocket to signal your sexual appetite. Color significance may vary from region to region, but one can be assured that red means one of two things: either 1) you like to stick an arm up a human rectum or 2) you like to have one stuck up yours. Yellow means you like to be used as a toilet (*de gustibus non est disputandem*). Blue means you like to cuddle, and white means you're into blowing your nose. Wearing red, yellow, blue, and white at the same time means you're indecisive, color blind, or desperate. Or questioning?

For footwear, work boots are deemed acceptable for any occasion, especially for evening wear, as they show an interest in the strivings of the lower classes and mark you as broad-minded. Open-toed sandals, however, are worn only in tropical climates by trans-peons. Cuban heels are worn only by midgets or Carmen Miranda impersonators.

Jewelry is out, except for a simple ring or a single small earring. More jewelry or more than one earring means you are running for Empress of Fresno.

You may wear a jacket, possibly leather or denim, but never wear it zipped up to your chin or wear matching ear-muffs, as these mean you are a nerd. Remember, if you dress properly, with everything in its place, you will attract any number of interested parties, who will wish to take you home and have sex with your attire.

 # HEALTH

~ stimulants

Here is a Brief Test so that you will be informed about drugs and thus be able to converse knowledgeably in any social circle. (The answers are at the bottom. Play fair. Don't peek now!)

DRUGS

1. You are square if you think Brownies are which of the following:

   a. homoerotic Negroes

   b. the pubic regions of Girl Scouts

   c. better than Sara Lee

2. Actors should do which:

   a. remember their lines

   b. snort them

   c. can they do both at the same time? NO!

3. You have just told the world's most marvelous joke. You are most likely:

   a. a professional comedian

   b. God

   c. smoking marijuana with friends

4. The cocaine connoisseur needs:

   a. a sterling silver razor blade

   b. a plastic nose

5. Nice addicts don't:

   a. shoot up in public

   b. overdose in class

   c. steal from grannies

   d. forget to clean their room

6. You have just seen a vision of the Virgin Mary. You are undoubtedly:

   a. saintly

   b. a peasant in Portugal craving attention

   c. on magic mushrooms

7. Police officers do not:

    a. plant drugs

    b. take bribes

    c. keep what they confiscate

    d. none of the above

Answers: 1 (a, b, or c); 2 (a and b); 3 (c); 4 (b); 5 (a, b, c, and d); 6 (c); 7 (d)

 # DEPORTMENT

PROPER CONDUCT OF THE GAY GENTLEMAN IN LEATHER BARS:

1. You may speak only when spoken to.

2. You will speak only to known individuals, such as your friends and the bartender.

3. Smiling at strangers is forbidden. (Eye contact is allowed, under certain circumstances.)

4. One thumb must be kept in at least one pocket at all times.

5. A hand on the hip means that you are not being careful.

6. A drink in one hand and a cigarette in the other means nobody will notice you're lonely.

PROPER CONDUCT OF THE LESBIAN GENTLEWOMAN:

1. A lesbian does not speak to a man she has not been introduced to.

2. Dresses are worn only by transvestites.

3. Slapping with an open palm is forbidden. (Punching out is okay, but only in bars.)

4. Aspiring to be "The Swan" on TV was and is a no-no.

5. There are simpler ways to become a Lesbian than to be a man who has a sex change and then "dates" women.

6. Even in jest never refer to your partner, whether male or female, as your Comfort Woman. No . . . no.

 # AN ABRIDGED LIST OF
VICES AND BLOTS UPON THE CHARACTER

1. People who live in glass houses shouldn't throw orgies.

2. The macho gay male should not give head with a toothpick between his teeth, as this tends to cause apprehension in his partner.

3. The fem gay man must not scream and carry on on Castro Street merely because one is newly liberated. (You will scare the horses.)

4. A blow job must be heartfelt, or one's sincerity will be questioned.

5. A guest at a formal orgy does not demand second helpings.

6. Lesbians may withdraw to the drawing room for a smoke and a chat *only* after the gentlemen present have given their permission.

7. A gentleman would be horrified at the thought of loitering in a place where he might overhear the private affairs of other gentlemen, such as in a bathhouse.

8. Cock is, without a doubt, one of the most difficult foods to eat gracefully, second only to corn on the

cob. And yet it is too delicious to forego the pleasure of it simply because one might make a mess. It is permissible to use the fingers while eating cock. Hold it lightly, possibly at both ends, and do not slurp, except at the end. Sometimes a paper napkin is used. (Martha Stewart is particularly illuminating in her many books on the subject.)

9. Not to welcome a man to one's room is to break a convention that has many years of strict practice to uphold it. It is a serious blunder in hotel etiquette and is therefore *never* done.

10. Self-introductions are not unknown at a hotel. Still, it is not wise to go beyond the usual civilities (and/or anal intercourse, protected of course) until you get to know the other individual (or individuals) better.

11. If a gentleman becomes interested in another gentleman, either in the hotel lobby or other areas, he may request the concierge to make the necessary introduction, or unzip his pants while passing in the other gentleman's vicinity.

12. It is very bad manners to have sex in the toilet of a moving airplane, unless the door is left open so that others might be entertained if they do not care for the in-flight movie.

13. It is even worse manners to have sex with terrorists before or after a hijacking, but especially *during*!

14. When traveling on a sleeping car, the person who has the lower berth has dibs on the night porter.

15. When propositioning a police officer in uniform, keep the voice low and modulated.

16. Homosexuals must never touch intimately or put their arms around one another, unless they are in large numbers or in dark rooms.

17. One does not give Junior Achievement Awards to chicken hawks.

PARTIES

~ how to let guests have the most fun

1. It is in exceedingly poor taste for persons to carry on an intellectual conversation at a present-day party.

2. A *salon* is a place where one has one's hair done. *N'est pas?*

3. Under no circumstances should a host ever introduce anyone to anyone else.

4. The music must be of maximum decibels, for guests, like children, should be seen and not heard.

5. It is not expected that one remember a single name if people should introduce themselves to others.

6. Being a wallflower is a form of meditation. And you are building characters by frequenting that bowl of dip.

7. Those persons who are dancing (though *you're* not) are not really enjoying themselves.

8. The louder the cackle the worse the gin.

9. It is a host's inalienable right to poison your liver with "festive" chemicals in the punch.

10. It is sophisticated to urinate in the punch bowl, but only in San Francisco.

11. One drink is okay. Two are *très* gay. Ten are AA.

12. The only good party is last week's.

13. There is such a thing as a good party without . . . your lover's friends.

14. Children of Lesbians should be seen and not heard. (Little Tyler's complete collection of Rita Mae Brown's cat mysteries can wait for another time.)

15. If the police come, your party is one of these: a) pushy, b) a success, c) to be featured on the TV show *Cops*.

16. Having sex in the guest room is acceptable if one brings one's own sheets.

17. Nobody in the world really wants to eat dead snails on tiny crackers.

18. Do not invite Ellen Degeneres and Anne Heche to the same party. (Anne *who*?)

19. Conversation at a party is the triumph of the cerebral over the unbearable!

🪽 TRUE CHARACTER

~ the real you

If you are gay, you may sometimes be accused of not being a 'real' man or a 'real' woman. Therefore, we have devised the following test to help you determine if you are one so that, with self-knowledge, you will always be at ease wherever you may be. A score of five on either scale is necessary to qualify.

IF YOU ARE A 'REAL' MAN, YOU

1. tell 'fag' jokes

2. are obsessed with 'fags'

3. plan to go on a diet real soon

4. have a heart attack by 55

5. don't mind them in the theater

6. don't kiss while you're getting fucked

IF YOU ARE A 'REAL' WOMAN, YOU

1. don't rape and pillage

2. are taken for granted

3. wanted those nine kids

4. love your new spring burqa

 # HINTS ABOUT WHAT NICE PEOPLE DO

1. A Lesbian-Separatist by accident in mixed company never swears at a gentleman for lighting her cigarette, however much she may be incensed by his thoughtlessness.

2. Lesbians should never dine with their gloves on. (But a catcher's mitt perhaps?)

3. A well-bred Lesbian should be careful how she refuses to dance with a female partner. Above all she must take care not to accept two female partners for the same dance. Many duels have resulted from such a lack of attention to detail.

4. When dining with friends who have hired help for the evening, if you desire sex with the servant, do not call out "Waitress!" in a crass way, as you would in a restaurant, but call her by her name, or, better still, hint discreetly that you wouldn't mind if she sat on your face.

5. Gay men, please note. Amyl nitrite at lunch is not a compliment to the chef.

6. He who sprinkles cocaine on the blintzes should have his hand slapped.

7. He or she who breaks wind at table may be excused until such time as he or she is prepared not to repeat the offense.

8. If you pass gas at a Speed Dating roundelay, all is not lost. You will be moving on in nine minutes or less.

9. In planning a picnic, create an interest, if possible, by proposing something to see in the neighbourhood – a lake, a waterfall, or picturesque *bushes*.

10. In your demeanor at a country party on Fire Island, steer clear between the Scylla of Cherry Grove and the Charybdis of The Pines.

11. A kindly individual hesitates to show photographs of one's tricks to guests in the presence of one's lover.

12. Personal hygiene becomes a fault when you douche at table.

 # FINESSING THE ZEITGEIST

~ the Holy Scriptures

Mores change and the modern gay person must keep abreast.

Thus —

THE NEW AND IMPROVED TEN COMMANDMENTS

1. I am the Lord thy God. Thou shalt not have false gods before me, even Fred Phelps of Kansas.

2. Thou shalt not take the name of the Lord in vain, but you can talk dirty in the confessional if it's mutual.

3. Keep holy the Sabbath Day. Cruise a church.

4. Honor thy Parents and Friends of Gays.

5. Thou shalt not kill, unless you're in the military or hate HOMOS.

6. Thou shalt not commit adultery, unless it's a three-way with your spouse.

7. Thou shalt not steal, except from large corporations.

8. Thou shalt not bear false witness against thy neighbor, unless you're a Vice Squad decoy testifying in court.

9. Thou shalt not covet thy neighbor's wife, although thy neighbor's not bad.

10. Thou shalt not covet thy neighbor's goods, though Rev, Jimmy Swaggart's ass makes a tempting target.

 # OUR HERITAGE

~ *a pride of gays*

No doubt there were gays on the Mayflower. There are even rumors about James Buchanan, our fifteenth President. Kings and queens, inventors and artists, football heroes and financiers – we are indeed everywhere. So be proud of your heritage. Hold your head up high, and if anyone puts you down, just work the names of these famous homonids into your conversation:

FAMOUS HOMOSEXUALS –

1. Achilles, who loved his Patroclus with a "cousinly" love rarely seen, if the movie *Troy* is to be believed

2. Alexander the Great

3. Alexander the So-So

4. Michelangelo (Mikey to his Pope friends)

5. Leonardo DaVinci (Lenny to his *boy*-friend)

6. E. M. Forster

7. Alice B. Toklas and Del Martin (before Gertrude Stein)

8. Dag Hammarskoldj (known as "Snoop Dag")

9. Sir Benjamin Britten

10. 8. Sir John Gielgud

11. 9. Sir Elton John

12. 10. John Maynard Keynes

UH . . . BEST NOT TO MENTION

1. Roy Cohn

2. Anne Heche

3. various Popes

4. Martha Stewart (but only when she served time as "Big Martha")

5. J. Edgar Hoover

6. Cardinal Spellman and other churchly figures

7. Lillian Smith, butch rival to ladylike Annie Oakley

8. Whitney Houston

9. Jeffrey Dahmer

10. I am not sure I quite approve of the flaming clown characters on TV's "Modern Family," a kind of gay Laurel and Hardy (if that is not redundant).

 # PROPER SPEECH

~ *handling rude homosexuals*

What does one say to someone who has been unkind? Should one return the unkindness? Should one be silent? Since downright bitchery is going out of style (or is that too optimistic?) what is left? Perhaps we can take a clue from our Middle-Eastern friends. For those special occasions when nothing else seems to suffice, try the expressions listed below. Don't use more than one per occasion, or you will be considered not only excessive but Third World.

GAY CURSES –

1. May all your erections wilt like week-old celery.

2. May you overdose on Viagra.

3. May your asshole shrink to the size of a dime under your hot lamp.

4. May your amyl nitrite turn to vinegar in your boyfriend's nose.

5. May you grow a third testicle, in a place no one can reach.

6. You should develop cataracts on your tits.

7. May your nephew accuse you of taking liberties with him at his Bar Mitzvah party.

8. May you wake up and find a transvestite knitting in your bed.

9. May internal parasites interfere with your yoga.

10. May a hyena French-kiss you while you're being crucified.

11. May your next trick make vile bubbles in your hot tub.

12. May you have sex with Howard Stern in the bushes.

13. May you lose to a hermaphrodite in a Mr. Macho Contest.

14. May your lover go straight.

15. May Osama Bin Laden haunt your brunch.

 # PROPER THOUGHTS

~ if you would remain in the company of your peers

THINGS THE GAY MAN DARE NOT ADMIT OUT LOUD

1. You are sexually attracted to femmes and fats.

2. You don't really like Maria Montez or Judy Garland.

3. You actually prefer to live in Toledo, Ohio.

4. You loathe brunches.

5. You hate big cocks, your own included.

6. You rather like Anita Bryant's singing voice and have all her albums.

7. You don't want to marry your long-term partner. (You'd settle for sex once in a while.)

THINGS THE GAY WOMAN DARE NOT ADMIT OUT LOUD

1. You are sexually attracted to secretarial work.

2. Barbie is not so bad.

3. They're not your sisters.

4. Abortion is killing a child.

5. You wish there were lesbians baths.

6. You think Gertrude Stein is hard to read.

7. There are higher literary standards than pulp fiction, past and present.

8. You're passive in life and that's okay.

 # WOMEN

~ *More Proper Thoughts*

1. Some gays are women, called *Lesbians*. (sometimes just *lesbians*)

2. Terms like *dyke* and *diesel* are used among the cognoscenti, but are not yelled from passing cars.

3. Lesbians do not like to be called "girls" or "sir."

4. If one of them wears men's pants and shirts, cuts her hair shirt, and lives in Alaska, she is known as a *Klondyke*.

5. Some lesbians think that some gay men are male chauvinists. Some gay men think that some lesbians are female chauvinists. Some just keep out of it, hoping it will pass.

6. Lea DeLaria is the lesbian Bob Hope. Bob Hope was the heterosexual Lea DeLaria. (Both once mingled with the troops.)

7. Miss America is almost never a lesbian . . . although Bert Parks used to be. (In case you don't know, Bert Parks also used to be the host of the Miss America Contest.)

8. Lesbian cheerleaders are known as Sapphettes.

9. Women's music festivals are never lesbian.

10. Lesbians are sometimes said to hate men, but in truth they only *dislike* them.

11. Lesbians generally are less concerned about appearance than gay men. Therefore, they are seldom asked to pose for gay porn magazines.

12. Lipstick Lesbians, however, often seem to appear in heterosexual pornography, because they want to make straight men like them, by making out with each other. (Ask Hugh Heffner!)

13. Women's history is sometimes known as *herstory*. When necessary, some women have hersterectomies.

14. Gay men often hug, kiss, and joke with their women friends. This is because they hate women.

15. Gay men sometimes date straight women. Gay women sometimes date straight women. (*Whatever.*)

16. Straight women who hang around gay men are sometimes unkindly called "fag hags."

17. Straight women who hang around straight women are called "housewives."

18. Straight women who hang around straight men are sometimes called "cunts."

 # COMING OUT

~ one cannot breathe for long in a closet

How do you reveal your gayness to Important Others in your life? For some, a face-to-face clarification is impossible. So consider the following letters and perhaps you can find the right words for you.

TO COME OUT TO PARENTS GENTLY

Dear Folks

Edgar and I will be coming to visit you next Sunday and Monday. He has a couple of days off from his job as a flight attendant, and I have some free time from the salon. We have something very important to tell you and hope that you will be as pleased as we are.

Does the extra bedroom still have my old single bed in there? (That should suit us just fine. Don't go to any fuss for us.)

Did you like the photograph that Edgar and I had taken at Fire Island?

How are things at the precinct, Dad?

Did you read where they rejected that gay rights ordinance somewhere? I guess some people just don't care about rights for other people, right?

Well, I guess that's about it for the news! See you soon.

Your only son

Hal

To Come Out to an Employer —

Dear Boss,

This is to inform you that your innuendos about "fruits" and "degenerates" have not gone unnoticed. This is also to inform you that I am not going to take your overcompensatingly macho remarks for another day, fathead.

No, I am not resigning, sir.

This is merely to inform you that the city council of this city has just passed an ordinance that prevents businesses such as yours from discriminating against the likes of

Yours Truly,

Warren Hunnicutt

TO COME OUT TO
THE UNITED STATES GOVERNMENT —

Dear Customs,

It has come to our attention that you have seized a gay publication from Sweden that I asked to be mailed to me. I called your office and asked for you to return said publication. (If you would consult File#H22578-90000001-43652-509R, you will, I'm sure, remember my earlier complaint.)

*Be advised that I have now **stopped** being nice.*

Be further advised that if I am not given back the publication in question within five (5) business days after receipt of this letter, I will send you a FOLLOW-UP letter that you won't soon forget. I do not mean to sound harsh or threatening, but who asked you to protect my morals?

I am sure that your staff is finished reading the offensive publication by now, and thus your office has no further need of it. I would appreciate its swift delivery to me, well thumbed or not.

Have I made myself perfectly clear? If you do not act soon, I will be forced to sic the gay Log Cabin Republicans on you. Believe me, you don't want the full force of so powerful an organization UNLEASHED AGAINST you.

Duane W. West

It is said that letters such as the following are no longer needed, but let's keep it as a reminder of how it used to be, and still is in too many places.

TO COME OUT TO
THE U.S. MILITARY —

To Whom It May Concern,

Forgive me for not writing sooner, but I have been recovering from my wounds suffered in the war in Iraq. It has been difficult for me to hold a pen or even use a keyboard. My partner (not business) is helping me with this letter.

I have just been notified that I am being discharged from the U.S. Army because I have violated the Don't Ask, Don't Tell policy. Apparently I screamed out my lover's name (Bill) when I was struck by shrapnel. Is it possible for you to make an exception in my case since I clearly did not intend to mention Bill's name since we are both close to twenty years of service and now neither of us will be getting his military pension.

If you rescind this order, I promise to continue to serve my country faithfully and never again discuss or even hint that I have unacceptable emotions or sexual desires – even if I'm captured and threatened with beheading by extremists. I know you may find it hard to believe that I can hold my tongue after what I have already done (in combat in Iraq and in this letter), but I assure you that I have had my tongue surgically removed while I have been here in the hospital. I was asked if I wanted to be surgically castrated, but may I please request that that be postponed until a later time, if it must come to that.

Awaiting hopefully your decision,

I remain

Captain Barney T. Wilesbarre

P.S. God bless the United States of America!

TAKING THE BATHS

~ *finding one's way in the maze of life*

Although gay baths have been shut down in some locations following the first edition of this book (1982), some still remain in operation, and so all the rules that must not be violated remain in force, with perhaps a few new ones added.

Towels should be knotted on the *left*.

A towel is not a sarong, and you are not Dorothy Lamour.

Don't overdo. Steam is good for you because it cleanses the pores, but it has been known to wilt the weenie.

One should not use the steam room right after a heavy meal. (Burping while fellating is just not acceptable, except on the Arabian peninsula.)

Staying too long in the sauna gives one a red face – and should!

If there is a maze, you may wander around in it, but if you get lost, do not call a policeman.

If the police still raid the baths in your part of the world, refuse to blow them, despite their demands, unless they shower first.

Don't reject someone on the basis of appearance alone. (Get to know the person. Then reject him.)

Leave your door open if you wish to have sex. — safe sex if now goes without saying. *Close* the door if you are just resting.

Lie on your back if you prefer to be fellated. Approach someone much better looking if you prefer to be *de*flated.

Lie on your stomach and tilt your derriere into the air if you wish to show a Whitmanesque openness to all mankind. (or if you are a total moron who has no sense of infections).

The TV Lounge is considered No Man's Land. (This is no aspersion on your masculinity.) Don't engage in sex here. Even more, don't use your cell phone. We are not interested in those plans for your next sexual conquest. Need we add that the camera in your cell phone is not to be used to capture *these* special moments.

Showers, like bath attendants, should work, at least occasionally.

Talking to a trick is permitted.

But your post-coital chats should be *interesting*, since the rest of us in our cubicles have to hear them too.

Slimy floors are not found in Nature.

If you over-stay your time limit, insist that your sheets be changed weekly.

If you have leprosy, do not use the Jacuzzi.

If you wish to sleep in the baths, try puncturing your ear-drums.

A heart attack in the steam room is Nature's way of saying: Go Home!

If you meet your closeted boss at the baths, it is considered rude to blackmail him into giving you a raise.

If you meet your father at the baths, tell him you're "just resting."

 # GLORY HOLES

~ Glorioski!

1. Corn on the cob is eaten sideways. Penises generally are not.

2. One does *not* tie a napkin around one's neck while dining at a glory hole.

3. One *may* raise a pinkie while lifting a male member for inspection.

4. Flicking away a male member as too small for one's consideration indicates inferior breeding, on whose part it is hard to say.

5. You don't have to be Gabriel to blow well.

6. Scribbling your name and phone number in ink on another's member does not provide a personal touch in an impersonal situation.

7. One does not have to accept *every* item offered one!

8. One may not pinch the merchandise like a low-class patron in a greengrocer's.

9. Equal rights demand that women be permitted to use glory holes, if they so desire.

10. Splinters in the tongue suggest lack of restraint.

11. Members of the Vice Squad are not allowed to come *before* they make an arrest, however much this rule may be broken in actual practice.

12. Toilet paper may not be used for party hats.

13. A tapping of the foot under the partition doesn't necessarily mean the other person is a chorus boy.

14. One penis at a glory hole is a welcome addition to a fretful day. Two at the same time at the same glory hole could be suspicious.

15. Teeth are for smiling — only.

INVITATIONS AND THANK-YOU NOTES

~ proper forms

There is entirely too much laxness in the form that people at present use for invitations and thank-you notes, handwritten of course, never by e-mail! Model yours scrupulously on the following examples.

AN INVITATION TO A PRIVATE PARTY

Dear Alf,

It was such a pleasure to meet you the other night at Tom's. I hope you remember me – I was the tall one in the leotards and the gender-fuck football helmet. I was very interested in your basket – the one you said you are weaving in your Personal Growth Therapy Class.

Perhaps you could show it to me sometime?

It might be fun for us to get together some night and just talk. All anyone seems to be interested in any more is sex, sex, sex! Maybe you wouldn't mind coming over to my place one night soon – perhaps this evening? – and we could discuss the terrible state of promiscuity among gay men.

Shall we say 8ish?

An Invitation
to Someone You Don't Like

Ralph,

You'll never guess – Pat and I are throwing a little get-together tomorrow night and so much want you to come.

Please excuse this late notice. I do hope it reaches you before the party is over, but you know how the Postal Service is! It would be a shame to miss your effervescent wit and cheery disposition. Who can ever forget how you regaled us with the details of your personal problems with mange at our last party!? You were on everybody's lips for weeks afterwards – especially the slides you brought.

Don't bring anything, as usual. Your presence is more than enough. We do hope you will delight us once again for another hour or two with those stories about corpses you've tricked with.

Love,

Bjorn

A THANK-YOU NOTE FOR A GIFT

Dear Amanda,

*Thank you a dozen times over for the lovely case of crabs you sent my way. They only just arrived. I can't tell you how thoughtful it was to send so many, as one hates running out, doesn't one? These should last me a good, long time. However did you find them? And the colors are so varied! You must have looked **everywhere** for them!*

Believe me, I will remember your for this.

Do Be in Touch,

Cindy

A THANK-YOU NOTE
TO A GAY ACTIVIST FUND-RAISER —

Dear Sirs,

I regret that I was unable to attend your recent fund-raiser for the National Gay Lobby. I'm afraid that I am not "into" politics.

Indeed, I think that gays have done quite all right up to now by minding their own business and staying where they belong. After all, we didn't have any trouble with the government, the police, the military, or the churches until all you activists started stirring people up! I really can't approve of all this carrying-on, when it's clear that, if we'd only just wait, the heterosexuals will give us what we want, as they always have.

What would Thomas Jefferson and Benjamin Franklin say if they could see people demanding their rights like this? (It's a dark day for a nation when its citizens have to riot and scream for their rights!)

Now . . . of course, when gays win complete freedom and full equality, feel free to contact me again. I may then be interested in doing what I can.

To the Future,

(Name Withheld)

 # CONCENTRATION CAMPS

~ nostalgia time

It has finally come to light that homosexuals were included in the Nazi concentration camps. It even appears that they were treated with special consideration by those in charge, and the other members of the camps likewise acknowledged their unique place there. How fortunate the gays were included. (It's sad but true that they have often been excluded elsewhere.) How nice to know that they were downright welcome at the concentration camps!

As we understand it, the homosexuals were treated to their own ceremony. Let's hope that some of charming customs won't be forgotten as time rolls along – and can even be repeated. So we have described below the affair as best we can, considering how little has been written on the subject.

Since coming to the camp was such a special occasion, the gays were always given a welcoming tea party, the tables set with pale blue or pink decorations, tasteful, never pretentious. Small doilies instead of one large tablecloth were customary. But the key to a successful tea party was unpremeditated simplicity, and those in charge often went to elaborate ends to achieve just such an atmosphere in camp.

Tea was Ceylon or jasmine. Sugar was hard to procure during those times. Still, the commandant always managed to provide at least some for the homosexuals. Tongs were used to put the sugar cubes into the tea. (**Tongs** and similar equipment were readily available in all the camps.)

Guests were usually served cream cheese and chopped walnuts or dates on raisin bread or baby watercress and very fine cucumber slices — nothing that would be too filling. Or they would help themselves from the tea wagon, always kept close at hand.

Dessert was traditional white cake with white frosting on which the gay inmates' names were written in pastel icing.

At such fetes, bonbons and ices were occasionally bypassed for the sake of war-time austerity, yet fresh flowers in vases were seldom omitted, it goes without saying. Unless a member of the clergy was present, the guests of honor sat at the head of the tables. Godparents were often surprise guests and sat at the inmates' side.

Bands of strolling musicians were always nearby to add to the festivities, though at some camps music had to be piped in, somewhat more mechanical but still thoughtful.

Gay men were expected to wear white trousers and dark sack coats with bright ties. Panamas were optional. The Lesbians present always wore silk, georgette, dotted Swiss, or crepe-de-chine, or something equally girlish and appropriate.

Since the guests were always brought in by special trains, they were often tired when they arrived. Thus the commandant rarely scheduled these affairs to last longer than a few hours. Even when he had gone out of his way, the commandant pretty much let the participants arrange their own games and didn't try to crowd too much entertainment into any one day. The commandant also did not make it a habit to attend these affairs himself, as, naturally enough, he had other pressing chores to attend to.

If the tea party began to extend into the evening, someone in authority would usually suggest that the party begin to taper off, because the new guests had to adjust to a new environment and probably needed a little time to themselves. Even the gayest gay needs his rest.

When the first day's frivolities were over and night was beginning to fall, the gays would turn on the gas in the lamps provided them and then retire to their . . . chambers.

🪽 CHOOSING THE PROPER MATE

~ *a little drama naturally*

Ah, to be in love! There's nothing quite like it, is there? It's a human experience not to be missed. Of course, you can't force something as delicate as *amour*. It must happen of its own accord. But if love does come to you, you must know how to act. The little play that follows is our way of dramatizing "Everything You Need to know About Finding a Mate."

CHARACTERS

Lover
Roommate
Venus
Beloved #1
Beloved #2

Lover

(in bathroom) Tonight's the night I fall in love! I can feel it in my bones!
(Applies roll-on deodorant to armpit)

Roommate

(getting a towel, angry because the Lover is taking so long) Well, don't bring home any goddamn drunken tricks at three in the morning, the way you did last weekend!

Lover

I don't know what you're talking about.

Roommate

I couldn't get into the goddamn bathroom because one of your numbers was puking in the toilet for an hour!

Lover

You have such a crude way of describing things.

Roommate

And I think the individual left crabs on the toilet seat besides!

Lover

(ignoring the Roommate) Tonight's the night! (Showing the roll-on) I'll have you know this contains Aluminum Sesquichlorohydrex!

Roommate

What's that?

Lover

An aphrodisiac.

Roommate

You don't need any. You need some saltpeter.

Lover

I need to fall in love.

Roommate

I hope you do. I need the sleep. (Exits)

Lover

(buttoning shirt) But I don't know if I can do it on my own.

(Venus appears)

Venus

You called?

Lover

Who are you and what are you doing in my bathroom?

Venus

I'm Venus, goddess of *amour*.

Lover

I don't believe you.

Venus

So fuck you, asshole. Who needs you? (Starts to leave)

Lover

Wait! Come back! (She comes partway back) Are you really Venus?

Venus

What do you think I am – some street hooker? (That's what she looks like)

Lover

How can I be sure?

Venus

Let me show you. (Comes over, raises her arms over her head) But first give me a shot of that deodorant with the aphrodisiac.

Lover

What?

Venus

(with arms still up in the air) Come on, come on! Roll some on me, honey.

Lover

(reluctantly rolling the deodorant on the armpit) Like this?

Venus

(grooving) Ooo, that's nice, baby! (Turns so that the other armpit can be done) Lay some more on me, stud!

Lover

(Does so) But it's supposed to be a man's deodorant.

Venus

Don't be narrow-minded, asswipe.

Lover

Is that enough?

Venus

(waving her arms like chicken wings, to dry the deodorant) Now I'm ready for anything! I haven't felt this good since I invented scabies.

Lover

You invented what?

Venus

Don't you know about my inventions? Passion, tenderness, venereal disease!

Lover

Venereal disease!

Venus

From Venus – venereal. Get it, Dum-Dum?

Lover

If you really are Venus, could you get me someone to love?

Venus

I might! What's it worth to you?

Lover

I'd do anything.

Venus

Will you sacrifice an ox?

Lover

Anything!

Venus

And burn it so the smoke drifts up to Mt. Olympus?
(She's grooving on the possibility.)

Lover

I promise! I promise!

Venus

(back to normal) Okay, what kind of love are you
looking for?

Lover

Is there more than one kind?

Venus

(takes out a brochure) Of course! You want to be
in love with somebody but with them not in love

with you? Or do you want somebody to be in love with you and you not in love with them? Or how about being in love emotionally but being impotent with the one you care for? Or maybe being sexually attracted to spiders? Or maybe –

Lover

Couldn't I just have somebody deeply in love with me and me in love the same way?

Venus

Is that all you can come up with?

Lover

I'll be satisfied with that. Honest.

Venus

Under her breath You wanna bet? (Moves over as if to do a magic trick) Okay, here goes. Wish real hard, asshole.

Lover

Mumbo-Jumbo! Jumbo-Mumbo! Alakazam! (Claps her hands) Behold – Beloved # 1!

Beloved #1

(looking at Lover) You asked for me?

Lover

You came?

Beloved #1

Not yet. Shall we? (Throws Lover to the ground, lies on top, and ruts) Isn't it wonderful? Are you having a good time?

Lover

Do you love me?

Beloved #1

(rutting harder) Oh, I love you! I love you with all my heart and soul, with all my insides and outsides, for now and forever!

Venus

Amen!

Lover

(freeing self with difficulty) No, I don't think this is the right person for me.

(Beloved #1 is still rutting in the same spot as though Lover is there.)

Venus

(angry) Why not?

Lover

I can't put it into words. (Looks at Beloved #1, who is still rutting and then starts to moan, then coming, then climaxing)

Venus

For Hades' sake, what more do you want?

(Beloved #1 eases off, sighs loudly, turns over on back. Goes to sleep, snores immediately)

Lover

I just don't think we're right for each other.

Venus

Christ, some people are never satisfied! (Snaps fingers and Beloved #1 rolls off and disappears) You only get one more try.

Lover

Only one more? But you said –

Venus

I haven't got all day to supply you with Beloveds. What about *my* sex life? I haven't had sex for minutes! You want me to *die*?

Lover

No, I just thought –

Venus

Make another wish, asshole!

(Lover wishes even harder this time, body shaking)

Lover

I'm wishing! I'm wishing!

Venus

(clapping hands) Here it comes – Beloved #2!

Beloved #2 (to Lover)

Hi!

Lover

Hi. How are you?

Beloved #2

Want to have breakfast together? (Arranges a table and two coffee cups)

(They hold hands, then sit at the table. Beloved #2 starts to read a newspaper)

Lover

Nice day, isn't it?

Beloved #2

(reading, not listening) Uh huh . . .

Lover

Gee, it's really great having a lover at last.

Beloved #2

(still reading) Uh huh . . .

Lover

(testing) I think I'm going to pour this hot coffee down the neck of your shirt.

Beloved

Uh huh . . .

Lover

(turning back to Venus) Venus!

Venus

Look, I can only arrange so much! After that, you're on your own.

Lover

(coming closer to her) But you promised me love!

Venus

Bitch, bitch, bitch! What have you done for me? I don't smell any oxen burning!

Lover

Do you want money?

Venus

Money can't buy love! On second thought, how much you got?

(Lover checks pockets.)

Lover

I seem to be broke at the moment.

Venus

I am!

Lover

Yeah, yeah, yeah!

Venus

I gotta go. (Starts to leave, to Beloved #2) Get lost, jerk. (Beloved #2 walks out, still reading the newspaper.)

Lover

But what about love!?

Venus

You had two chances, pal.

Lover

But I want what I've heard about in books and in songs!

Venus

(singing) "Love is a many-splendored thing!"

Lover

But where can I find it? Tell me! Tell me! Before you leave!

Venus

(starting to exit, singing) "Love makes the world go 'round! Love makes the world go 'round!"

Lover

Tell me the magic formula! Please!

Venus

(exiting, singing) "Can't forget, don't regret what I did for love!"

Lover

Venus, please! (Goes after her but stops short.)

Roommate

(passing Lover upon entering) Are you still in the bathroom? Excuse me, I've got to get ready. I've got a heavy date.

Lover

(sadly) Sorry . . . (Goes over and sits at the table.)

Roommate

(looking back, combing hair) What's the matter? I thought you were going out?

Lover

Naw, I think I'll stay in tonight.

Roommate

Suit yourself.

(Lover nods, lights slowly begin to fade.)

Lover

Yeah, I think I'll stay in tonight.

Fade Out

COMING-OUT PARTIES

~ balls (see also "testicles")

It is very much to the credit of the younger generation that, even before fathers began to balk at the expense of a traditional coming-out ball for their lesbian daughters, the debutantes themselves decided that it was folly to spend a small fortune on such a party, ostensibly to introduce them to society in which they already had been circulating for several years with the greatest ease.

And so, within the past few years, the lavish individual coming-out lesbian debutante party has practically disappeared, replaced, as we all know, by the collective Les-Deb Ball, during which fifty or a hundred young debs are presented all together, with the proceeds going to some worthy charity.

While each official lesbian debutante also gives a party of her own, it is on a much smaller scale than during the era of Brenda Frazier, who undoubtedly was the most publicized debutante (lesbian or otherwise) of all time. Moreover, it may even be a tea dance instead of a ball, or perhaps a luncheon followed by dancing, a dinner dance, a late supper dance, or just a meeting (with dance) at Daughters of Bilitis.

In the provinces of France and England, it is customary to give one party in London or Paris and another in the country, just as a Houston society woman might give one party for her les-deb daughter in that city and a more informal one in Palm Beach. An outdoor dance under tents is also always pleasant (although one must be alert to possible police raids).

The chief purpose of present-day debutante balls is to make it possible for the young lesbian to gain the acquaintance of other lesbians, of whatever age, so that she might form a Meaningful Relationship with one of them thereafter. Those who dance well at such occasions naturally enough stand the best chance of snaring a mate, inasmuch as dancing well has always been the single most important component in making a Meaningful Relationship last. (Recent studies have proven conclusively that dancing prevents Lesbian Bed Death.)

The second reason for such a debutante ball is so that the deb's proud family can formally present her to society as a lesbian. The atmosphere nowadays is gayer than it used to be, and there is far less ceremony and solemnity than there was during lesbian-coming-out parties in, say, the nineteenth century. Nevertheless, it is essentially a conventional affair and should be organized in the *traditional* way if is to be elegant. This is not the time for novelties in dress or decorum.

If you invite role-playing women to your debut, make sure that you have two separate receiving lines, one for femmes and one for butches. You may move back and forth between the lines to greet the guests, but make none of them feel uncomfortable. Do not, for instance, snub those who wear cosmetics, and also a gracious deb makes each butch feel like the bull of the ball. The honored lesbian debutante wears a white dress with long white gloves, or a tuxedo, whichever feels right for her.

Engraved formal invitations should be sent out at least three weeks in advance, and as much as two months in advance in cities where the lesbian deb season is very active. It may be necessary to check the date with other debs in order to avoid scheduling coming-out balls on the same evening, as one would not wish to take attention away from a deserving honoree.

Mothers who take this sort of activity as seriously as they should will go to a great deal of trouble and expense and play a great deal of social politics to insure that their lesbian daughters have a brilliant "season." Unless your social, position and connections are impeccable, it would be advisable to enlist the aid of a more powerful society matron (or possibly the National Gay Task Force) if you wish to launch your darling daughter in a truly fitting blaze of glory.

BEING WELL-INFORMED

~ your brain can be hung too

Have you ever tried to carry on a conversation with a person who was not well-informed? Not very much fun, was it? But have you ever thought that maybe, just maybe, you aren't as well-informed yourself as you might be? Of course you have — because you are an individual who cares about the impression you make on others.

Well, one topic that never fails to make for sprightly talk is that of **Famous Persons of the Past and Present**. If one lacks information about everything else in the entire world of knowledge, one can always make a dazzling figure with tidbits about those who are, or have been, in the spotlight.

Try our little test and see just how much you are **In The Know**. If you don't do well, perhaps it's time you did something about it!

1. Anita Bryant, who led the Save Our Children campaign against gays in the1970s is:

    a. now working as a waitress in a McDonald's in Reno

    b. still filled with the glory of the Lord

    c. still full of something else

2. Eminem is:

    a. The rapper from Detroit who bashed gays in his early songs

    b. The rapper who defends a gay character in his first movie 8 *Mile*.

    c. The Pat Boone of rap

3. Sex with Liberace must have been the nearest thing to:

    a. coming with God Almighty

    b. eating a thousand pounds of white sugar in one sitting

    c. a piano's nightmare

4. Gore Vidal was endowed like:

    a. King Kong

    b. Tom Thumb

    c. most colleges

5. Quentin Crisp was or is:

    a. buttered and eaten with tea

    b. in the re-make of Auntie Get Your Gun

    c. posing nude in Heaven

6. History's all-time least favorite "trick" is:

    a. Attila the Hun

    b. Father Damien of Molokai

    c. John Wayne Gacy

7. Montgomery Clift was:

    a. called Princess Tinymeat behind his back

    b. married to Elizabeth Taylor

    c. married to James Dean

    d. never married

8. E. M. Forster wrote:

   a. all his books before the age of forty-five

   b. with a quill, on Thursdays

   c. about "tricking" with Indians

   d. under the pen name of Sarah Orne Jewett

9. Tennessee Williams, after his memoirs appeared, lived:

   a. in Key West

   b. it up

   c. it down

10. President George W. Bush died:

   a. in a Hummer accident on a surprise visit to Iraq to see the boys

   b. from a barrage of shots by a contingent of gun owners unhappy that he wasn't implementing the Anti-Gay Marriage Amendment fast enough

   c. from a Weapon of Mass Destruction

11. Felice Picano is writing:

   a.   a book that isn't about people with lots of disposable income

   b.   his mother regularly

Answers: (We'll never tell.)

 # PROPER SPEECH

~ *dishing and put-downs*

No doubt there is much greater freedom for the gay person at the present time. However, a few words about license in speech may still be in order. One must remember that, although free to speak out as never before, one must draw the line at an unruly tongue. (A *ruly* tongue, of course, is quite another matter.) To see if you are fit to mingle in good company, complete the following. A score of two or more means you need to revamp your pubic image. (Er, make that *public* image.) (Of course we assume you do watch your *pubic* image as well.)

SELF-EVALUATING BITCH TEST

Choose one answer as the most likely you would say:

1. Your best friend has just begun a new romantic relationship. You say:

    a. You sure know how to pick 'em!

    b. I'm only sorry you saw him first.

    c. I give it two weeks!

2. The pastor of your Metropolitan Community Church wears an expensive new purple vestment during the service. You say:

    a. your prayers

    b. Gee, Ted looks great in purple!

    c. Who does she think she is, Her Holiness?!

3. The Virgin Mary appears to you in a vision. You say:

    a. What took you so long?

    b. Come on, honey. I remember you *before* you were a virgin.

    c. Hi, Mary! Getting' much?

MAKE-UP / PLASTIC SURGERY

~ the heartbreak of hit-and-run cosmetic surgery

Some gay men (to say nothing of lesbians) are afraid to use make-up because they think it will take away from their masculine image. But really now, ask yourself — does wearing eye-shadow necessarily mean one is femme? Fellows, you must get over that negative conditioning. Did yau know that it has recently come to light that some very famous men have worn eye-shadow? Dwight D. Eisenhower, for example, was known to favor Estee Lauder. Indeed, Dwight and his brother Milton both used to wear it to family gatherings. (Source: Wikipedia)

Moreover, Frederick the Great and J. Edgar Hoover were noted in their day for wearing mascara and still managed to starts wars and keep files on subversives, so why shouldn't you? (But enough of this canard about J. Edgar in drag. He wore it only on festive occasions at the FBI.

If you are running for national office, keep your eye make-up to a tasteful minimum, as too much may perhaps cost you some votes in Arkansas.

Remember that your mascara must be waterproof, or else it dribbles in the steam room. And false eyelashes are out, unless you happen to have lost yours because of some dreadful disease, the details of which no one cares to hear.

As for your eyebrows, do not make the arch too pronounced or you may be mistaken for Gale Storm. (If you don't know *My Little Margie* there is no hope for you, and you must turn in your Gay Card.)

Who says you're not masculine if you tweezer your eyebrows! Those people haven't the faintest idea how much pain tweezers can cause. To use them you must be tougher than General George Patton or at least as tough as Courtney Love. And as for facial astringents – why, they're practically a form of S&M!

Don't tell us about manliness! Masculine you will be, if you wear *manly* make-up! There's nothing effeminate about powder, lipstick, and rouge!

The important thing is to maintain a natural look. A little pancake make-up goes a long way, boys. (Otherwise you look like Death in Venice or Pee-Wee Herman.)

Go easy on the darkest bronzing gel too, men, because smeared pillows the morning after do not for true love make. Never apply it directly below the eyes either and avoid blush-on products, as these tend to make you look like you are starring in a minstrel show. But tell me why a person, just because he or she happens to be over sixty-five, should have that pale look when they can look utterly natural with help!

Don't tell us that people with bronzed faces look artificial! What nonsense! (Of course some bronzing gels do look too orange or too yellow, giving you that chronic hepatitis look. Avoid these, if you *would* trick.)

If the gel still leaves some zits or discoloration showing, you might try Erase, the Max Factor cover-stick. If that doesn't work, you might try surgery, but be certain the doctor comes highly recommended, or you could learn the heartbreak of hit-and-run cosmetic surgery. Some of the newer laser treatments are splendid, as long as you do not get them at a Seven-Eleven store.

Now obviously you won't rush into any of this, as some have done, just for mere physical attractiveness. Can you imagine such shallowness! Never, never never!

Never!

For the lips a natural lip gloss is best, although dock workers look good in any shade of Elizabeth Arden pink. (It catches the sun so nicely as it comes up over those wharves.) Use Chapstick in a pinch, but, remember, it makes a poor lubricant anywhere but on the mouth.

If you decide to have you face lifted, don't let those black eyes bother you one bit. You can tell your friends you got them sparring with Muhammad Ali.

Besides, they will go away in no time and you will look marvelous. (People probably won't even recognize you!)

A body overhaul sometimes goes well with a face-lift. You can take care of the entire package at once. A snip here or there, some tightening, some collagen, and – presto – you're macho! (Don't neglect that testosterone shot, just to be sure.)

. . . Now let's be deadly serious for a minute, guys. When should you give up and throw in the trowel, so to speak? We'll tell you when – Don't ever, ever say "To Hell with it all!" There's no reason in this world why, when you're ninety-two, you can't, with effort, look seventy-two! Just never say never!

Think back when having your hair styled and carrying a bag were considered feminine. Well, soon make-up will be just as butch as jockstraps and fag-baiting. Come on, you're not sissies. You on the front lines of fashion, soldiers!

 # CORRESPONDENCE

~ *answering "those" advertisements*

PEN PALS

It may happen that there will be a time in your life when you are lonely and may want to meet people. You can meet some people at parties, at bars, in back rooms; still, experts say that advertising in a gay publication can bring instant results. Look at the following ads from one of our better-known newspapers and model your own accordingly. (Needless to say, you may answer any of these ads that appeal to you.)

1. W/M prisoner, 24, wants to meet human being. Any age. For conjugal visits. Discreet. Write: Ron, Box 82, Vacaville, CA.

2. Open, easy-going W/M seeks lover. No fems, fats, uglies, shorties, ethnics, allergies, introverts, extroverts, drinkers, smokers, activists, or fools. Must be employed, under thirty, over nine inches, and own your own car. Send photo. Box 191, Kitchener, Ontario.

3. Devoted, loving W/M seeks sincere, permanent relationship with male any age. Must be wealthy. Call Matthew: 921-0091.

4. Hot Topman , 92, seeks hunky dudes with toys. Can you take it, Mister? Contact Pops: 432-8975.

5. Rip-Off Massage Service. Youthful males to tend to your every need and relax you in your own home. Easy payments. 900-989-7000.

6. Handsome, Sexy, Hot Super-Hung Hunk. *Playgirl* discovery. Shy. Modest. Seeks lover. Call Brad: 596-3400.

7. Anglo-German G/M, 29, seeks North Africans for Greek passive/French active. Translator provided. Eric: 211-3344.

8. B/M, 52, enjoys drinking Kool-Aid, watching "Laverne and Shirley" re-runs, collecting old lace, playing Old Maid. Like to get to know you better. Call Wimpy: 632-3653.

9. G/B/F tired of bar scene, looking for G/B/F into dancing and excessive drinking at home. Contact Pam: 556-6079.

10. Bisexual biker wants butch women into handcuffs and scat and sissy men into cock piercing and flower arranging. Your place or

mine. No kooks. Terry: Ad # 3999, care of this paper.

11. Interested in forming gay commune. Like to cook. Eight lacto-vegetarians looking for stable environment. Have own goat. For the Kollective write Mark: RR No. 1, Red Neck, Oregon.

12. G/A/M, 37, 6′ 8″. Eunuch. Seeks person who values a spiritual relationship. Call collect: Sok U: 865-676-0985.

13. MASSAGE. Bobby makes outcalls. Call Bobby to make out: 871-2229.

14. 450 lb. blue-eyed Transsexual into Inner Child Therapy and junk foods. Versatile. Willing to re-locate. Call Thalia: 987-1001. (Remember: Thalia won't fail ya!)

15. Hair fetishist will do your hair. Wash & Set. Styling. Blow dry. $45. Maxie: 986-8854.

16. Blue-haired Senior Citizen from northern Red State wants help shoveling snow off sidewalk. No sex. Minimum wage. Winters only. Mrs. Connie Walsh: 357-0012.

17. Morals Values Preacher wants rim job, either way. So bad it hurts. Contact: Rev. X, P.O. Box 3456789, Holy Baptism, Mississippi.

SPORTS; PART TWO

If you don't like sports, you must nevertheless make an effort to be interested when others are discussing athletics, as when standing in supermarket lines or eating a holiday dinner in the company of your sister's husband.

Here are some samples of **Lively Expressions** to use in order to give at least the appearance of interest, which is all they can reasonably expect! (The teams mentioned are entirely fictitious.)

1. Say, did you hear! The Texas Lubes creamed the Los Angeles Hot Dogs.

2. The Toronto Tomboys whipped the ass of the Boston Puritans, 9-1.

3. A night game held in Central Park ended in a stunning triple- play. (Tinky Winky to Evers to Chance), although fans agreed it was risky to leave anything to Chance.

4. Last night the New York Hustlers traded several players, as yet unnamed, to the Long Island Financiers, for an undisclosed amount of cash.

5. This just in: The San Francisco Butches licked the pants off the Oakland Ladies Auxiliary.

6. The Blind Boys of Tennessee beat off the U.S. Senate.

7. In a surprising upset, the St. Louis Nances trounced the Montreal Studs.

8. The Athens Gays blew a lead to the Spartan Gays 4-2.

9. The Vatican Cardinals out-manned the Lisbon Feminists 270-0.

10. The Santa Monica Blackmailers toppled the Hollywood Closets, as expected.

11. The last-place Milwaukee Masochists surprised the Seattle Sadists by thrashing them 21-2.

12. The Atlanta Decoys threw a forward pass to the Southern Patsies.

13. A minor league team, the Pittsburg Pederasts, has applied for recognition by the baseball commissioner. Acceptance is not expected.

AND . . .

14. Last Sunday the Dallas Dykes plastered the Women's Christian Temperance Union, 30-0.

15. The Fire Island Trendies took on the Provincetown Regulars in a day-night double-header that became a free-for-all. Charges were dropped.

16. Over the weekend the East Hampton Queens bought and paid for the Harlem Foxes.

17. The Folsom Street Slaves tied with the Folsom Street Kinks in the Masters Tournament in Hula Hooping.

18. The Houston Globetrotters scored heavily against the Bangkok Chickens.

 ASTROLOGICAL SIGNS

~ what sign are you!?

Some people may call astrology bunk, but it does not pay to ignore a possible source of information, however uncertain. God knows, life is difficult enough without spitting on horoscopes. We should take any speck of help we can get, yes? Besides, if it was good for the astronomer Ptolemy, then it's good enough for me. On top of that, we can't always rely on logic to guide our lives, or where would the fun be?

Therefore, read the following descriptions of the signs of the Zodiac carefully and apply them as the need arises. (Thank you, Linda Goodman.) Remember, in social situations of all types, compatibility is the key.

THE GAY ZODIAC

ARIES
(MARCH 20 – APRIL 20)

Aries are usually out-going, frank, and incapable of cunning, except when they are weak, mealy-mouthed, and sneaky. (They are most often the latter when they have turned from being your lover to being your ex.)

You can notice the sign of the ram in the heavy brows, and they tend to be hung like goats. (If you date them, be careful not to be arrested for bestiality.)

They often suffer from raging fevers, fulminating infections, high blood pressure, and strokes. They are also subject to skin rashes, painful kneecaps, and stomach disorders. (They are always optimists, but of course they depress *you* by having so many ailments.)

TAURUS
(APRIL 21 – MAY 21)

Taurus is the bull. Look for a ring in the nose and a reluctance to date Spaniards. The females tend toward the bovine (though we dare you to tell *them* that).

All of them are stoic and stubborn, confining their arguments to monosyllables, as in "Yep," "Nope," "Thanks," and "Bye." (The males are often backroom "tricks.")

They seek a connection with the land, and, being an earth sign, they like sex to be dirty.

Taureans must watch their weight, and gout is a possibility, as is bankruptcy from getting hooked on Mrs. See's candy creams.

Every Taurean owns some evidence of the Venusian love for art and music. Most of them have Diana Ross albums up the ass.

Tease them too much and be prepared for a strong reaction.

(Hitler was a Taurus.)

GEMINI
(MAY 22 – JUNE 21)

The twins of the Zodiac are notable for their changeable personality. They prefer to skip back and forth in everything, making it difficult to live with them if you're into possessiveness. They usually disguise their true motives and use aliases, so when you receive a letter from one of them, often you don't know who wrote it, but at least you got a letter!

They take mischievous delight in disconcerting slower minds and also resent drudgery and monotony. If you're into drudgery and monotony or have a slow mind, avoid Geminis.

They often have receding hairlines and dual desires, especially if they're born on the cusp, in which case they are bisexual and tend to brag about it to excess.

CANCER
(JUNE 22 – JULY 23)

The crab. The best time to hunt for crabs is by the light of the natal moon (or with a flashlight, if that's closer). But whatever you use, don't delay! Crabs multiply in *those* places faster than sin.

Cancerians are subject, like the tides, to highs and lows. When depressed, they can be lower than the ocean floor. (If busted by the police, beaten up by street punks, or fired from their jobs for being gay, they act like real *crybabies* and go off and sulk.)

A Cancerian reveres the past, so be careful if he stays out at night – he may be tricking with his ex. Cancer also loves history and collects antiques. If it's old, it has value. If it's new, it's suspect. (Gay men past eighty will do well to seek out the company of Cancerians.)

You can recognize Cancerians because they are a distinct physical type: they have four legs and two pincers.

The crab is never impulsive and lunges only when it seems that someone else is about to get the prize. (Watch them just before closing time, or they will get that hottie you've been eyeing all evening.)

Cancerians practically invented ulcers, suffer from chills, and must watch their kidneys and bladder. (Because nobody else is going to watch 'em.)

LEO
(JULY 24 – AUGUST 23)

There are no introverted Leos. You can tell one by the way he elbows his way past you in any check-out line. Some Leos mellow with age, but the lion never really changes his spots.

The lioness of this sign will look you right in the eye and tell you with a slightly superior manner exactly how you should manage your life. (She's either a Leo or a group therapy graduate, *summa cum laude*.)

Leos are wildly extravagant, like to gamble, and are romantic. (You've been warned!) They also drive out fading male competition, kill their cubs, and mate with the leftover females. (A Disney movie it ain't.)

They have either very strong hearts or weak ones, except when they've had heart transplants, in which cases: See other signs.

The lioness is always ready to pounce if she feels threatened. (Ask her about Affirmative Action. Go ahead, ask her! If you are a white male, to subdue her simply give her your job.)

VIRGO
(AUGUST 24 – SEPTEMBER 23)

Marriage is not a natural state for the Virgin nature, so don't marry one if you live in a state that forbids gay marriage. (How many is it now?)

Virgos are not gregarious and are uncomfortable in crowds. (They hate visiting The Third World and are even more distressed that The Third World seems to be moving where they are.)

People of this sign are selective and precise in grooming, eating, working, and romancing – or, if you don't like Virgos, you could say that they are fussy, hypercritical, and anal retentive. (The latter is still preferable to the anal propulsive!)

Since they're not much into sex, one of life's greatest treasures is a blow-job from a Virgo . . . or whoever.

At their best they are dependable and gentle. At their worst they are nuns with large paddles.

Vulcan types are often vegetarians, or at least extremely concerned about diet and health. They are experts about herbal teas, millet, twelve-grain breads, bran, and brewer's yeast. (They make terrible Christmas dinners but excellent witches.)

LIBRA
(SEPTEMBER 24 – OCTOBER 23)

The scales, Libra tries to weigh everything until it is just right. Fairness is their fetish. They are also doubtful and fickle, frustratingly inconsistent.

Gay males Libras sometimes married to straight women, and lesbian Libras are sometimes married to straight men. This is because they are Libras, or possibly because they are movie stars.

The Libra is first up, then down. (This is bad news when it gets to impotence.)

But the women are invariably pretty and the men handsome. (Libras also are the ones who write these horoscopes.)

He/She doesn't really care which side he/she takes in an argument, as long as it is the *other* side. These people also balk at taking orders. (They make absolutely terrible M's!)

Libra is an air sign, and you will often find their legs up in it.

Scorpio
(October 24 – November 22)

The scorpion. More U.S. presidents have been born under this sign than any other. Nevertheless, you can overcome this tendency and be your own person if you don't really want to be president.

The typical Pluto person has a pale complexion and a heavy growth of hair on the arms and legs, often of a reddish cast (and tends to be born in Ireland and not to be female).

Impervious to both insults and compliments, these souls proudly and consciously practice a blank expression. (They frequent gay leather bars in *droves*.)

Scorpios must be careful to avoid fire, explosions, noxious fumes, and radiation. (Who shouldn't?)

The parts of the body governed by this sign are the reproductive organs. Scorpios tend to be active sexually and have been known to wear out nine dildoes in three days. They make poor conversationalists and restless dorm-mates – but excellent stag movies.

SAGITAURIUS
(NOVEMBER 21 – DECEMBER 21)

The archer shoots his arrows free of malice and is surprised when people scream that they've been hit. Sagittarius speaks and acts first and considers the consequences later.

This is a fire sign, and many Sagittarians are extroverts or arsonists, or both.

They love animals passionately, and their symbol is the centaur. In fact, most of them have a stray lock of hair on their forehead, like a horse's mane. (Occasionally, some act like a horse's ass.)

They are attracted to danger and have been known to cruise Mafia bars. (They do all right, too.)

Sagittarians seek the stage but can't tell jokes very well, so they usually act as Master of Ceremonies at wedding receptions in the Midwest.

At their best, Sagittarians are charming, cheerful, witty, and physically captivating. (They always have monogamous relationships with somebody other than *you*.)

Capricorn
(December 22 – January 20)

The goat likes to climb. (It's in his rising sign.) Very often indeed Capricorns are social climbers. They court success, respect authority, and honor tradition. They make good groupies and bad hippies. When they overdo this trait, they marry for money or social position. Beware of hustlers who are goats.

By sheer doggedness (or goatedness) Capricorns win out. They may seem to merge into the group, camouflaging themselves, but they outlast the flashier types and succeed.

Unfortunately they have melancholy dispositions and suffer from psychosomatic paralysis and mental distress. Public scenes and raw passion embarrass them, so they are very boring at orgies. But they make great coffee afterwards.

AQUARIUS
(JANUARY 21 – FEBRUARY 19)

Aquarius (the age which we have now entered) respects individuality, equality, brotherhood, love for all, and the philosophy of live and let live. (Ayatollahs and other fundamentalists have an afflicted Aquarius, it would seem.)

Uranians delight in shocking more conventional people and often adopt weird attire to show their refusal to conform. (Gender-fuckists and women who won't wear *chador*, you can bet on it!)

Often Aquarians evidence feminine characteristics in the male (The Rev. Oral Roberts, for instance) and masculine characteristics in the female (the shoulders of Joan Crawford).

They have great sympathy for mental defectives but do not believe credit cards should be issued to them, except when they are from socially prominent families.

They seek quantity rather than quality in their associations. (*Terrible* size queens, some of them.)

PISCES
(FEBRUARY 20 – MARCH 19)

The typical Neptune heart is free of greed . . . but you'd better watch them with the liquor. Pisces is a water sign, but they prefer it fermented. They'll ferment Kool-Aid if you'll let them. They must refrain from stimulants or sedatives of any kind.

Pisces are usually touchy and may tend to cry when you slap their hands as they go for your medicine cabinet.

Piscean eyes are liquid, heavy-lidded, and full of strange lights. (These are either bedroom or fish eyes.)

In general they are sweet, sensitive, and enjoy having their bodies stroked. They make good pets. But their rooms sometimes smell like zoos.

 # GIFTS

~ what does one give

It is better to give than to receive (although active is not necessarily superior to passive). But what to give, that's the rub. (Of course you might *give* a rub if the other party is interested.) Yes indeed, knowing exactly what to give for those birthdays, those holidays, those special occasions can cause you to wrack your brain for days attempting to come up with something appropriate, something personal, something that shows exactly how you feel. To take the agony out of decision-making, we have compiled a list of perfect presents. And you may rest assured that the gifts here designated are always impeccably correct.

GIFTS IN THE BEST TASTE

1. For those in prison for "sex crimes" that are not *now* considered crimes – 75 cents compensation and a framed apology from the parole board on genuine bond paper

2. For your friends going to Asia for the first time – a list of *non*-hustler bars and a quick return ticket

3. For the lover with whom you parted on good terms – cancellation of that restraining order and a three-way with your new lover

4. For the lover with whom you parted on bad terms – a six-months' supply of hemorrhoids

5. For the Nazi of your choice – a week's stay at Hitler's country place

6. For your ex-lover's wedding present – a half-membership in the Club Baths

7. For your sister's ninth baby shower –a manual on self-control and a stopper

8. For the minister of your choice who encourages his congregation to oppose gay rights – a Do-It-Yourself Brain Transplant Kit

9. At Christmas time. For the cultured fundamentalist art lover on your block – a picture of the Last Supper painted on genuine black velvet

10. 10. For your friend with chronic hepatitis – an all-expenses-paid trip to Lourdes

GIFTS IN THE BEST TASTE

1. For your friend's 80 birthday – an Accu-Jac and a lifetime subscription to a muscle magazine

2. For your drag cousin in Fort Wayne, Indiana – forty Barbra Streisand albums and a booklet on how to lip-synch (maybe a book on how *not* to lip-synch?)

3. A copy of Nolo Books' *Easy Divorce* for your gay friends so eager to get legally hitched

4. A framed death certificate for your co-worker killed cruising the *mujahideen*

5. An adoption application for your gay couple friends wishing to adopt a Russian child and save it from being Russian – with the pages glued together, to save them the heartbreak.

KINKY SEX AND AMUSEMENT

S&M

1. The Servant Problem: Now this is only a problem when somebody wants you to be his servant and you don't want to be. A simple "No" won't do here – be forewarned! For some may say "No," but there's "Yes, Yes" in their eyes. The wisest thing to do if you are forced into a collar against your will – that is, *really* against your will. You can see how complicated this gets – is to hit him in the nuts. That's how he will know to "respect your limits."

2. Designer chaps strike some as affected.

3. The true butch wears only imported leather.

4. Mad cows make marvelous leather adornments, once sterilized

5. But leather is not *de rigueur* except on elderly cows

6. Remember, no matter what anybody says, S&M is theater, and we all need a good laugh now and again.

7. Nipple-piercing is recommended for those who don't have enough troubles already.

8. Hoods may be worn whilst torturing another (or in inclement weather) but never with a cape.

9. Tattoos are fine, but swastikas are tacky.

10. If anyone sneers at you for wearing silly costumes, beat the person to death.

11. Racks are not required, except on very formal occasions, or holydays.

12. Those who spurn tit-clamps and crucifixions are old fuddy-duddies.

13. Giggling is not permitted during branding.

SCAT

1. If you don't know, don't ask!

2. If God meant us to smear shit on each other, He wouldn't have given us the Middle East instead.

3. If God had meant us to eat shit, Colgate would put it in tubes.

4. Shit should not be eaten unless it is properly chewed, 28 times per bite, *n'est pas*?

5. How do you know you won't like the taste if you won't even *try* it?

6. With the plethora of people posting Before pictures of their food on Facebook, let us be

grateful for the small mercy that they do not often post After pictures as well.

WATER SPORTS

1. A drink of urine is not a love potion to all.

2. Piss has very little nutritional value, advocates to the contrary.

3. Things go better with Coke.

4. A piss on the hand may be quite Continental.

5. Good manners demand that bathtubs be used for baths.

6. Thirsty dude with six-pack, don't call us; we'll call you.

7. Good Catholics do not drink piss during Lent. (E-piss- copalians may.)

8. A polite host will not pee on his guest without first asking.

9. Water Sports have given new meaning to piss-elegant.

10. What do you give a man who has everything? A Water-Pic with a catheter?

11. Remember when peeing in bed meant you hadn't grown up yet?

12. The International Olympics Committee does not recognize Water Sports, although it is leaning that way.

13. That statue of that little boy in Belgium started the whole thing. (One man's kitsch is another man's child pornography.)

 # HOW TO TELL

~ ah, romance

It looks, feels, and tastes like love, but is it? Answer: YES or NO to the following and find out. You wouldn't want to make any mistakes in this crucial part of your life, would you? Ten YESES and it's the real thing. Less than ten . . . keep on trying.

1. You don't mind his cock tattoo.

Yes ○

No ○

2. You don't mind talking about his ex-lover.

Yes ○

No ○

3. You had one evening out and two meals together without sex of any kind.

Yes ○

No ○

4. You have memberships in the same gym, which neither uses.

Yes O

No O

5. You didn't rim on the first date.

Yes O

No O

6. He didn't give you anything except attention.

Yes O

No O

7. You didn't write your name and telephone number on a scrap of paper. (You used a full sheet.)

Yes O

No O

8. The sex wasn't that fantastic, but you remembered his name.

Yes O

No O

9. He said he'd like to see you again (and actually called).

Yes O

No O

10. Oddly enough, he's not your "type."

Yes O

No O

11. You didn't want to go out and have sex right after he left.

Yes O

No O

12. You feel easy (and uneasy), apprehensive, happy (and unhappy), clean, and valuable.

Yes O

No O

13. Twenty years have gone by and you still haven't kicked him out.

Yes O

No O

SAMPLE GREETING CARDS TO SEND

STYLISH

Fuck you on Xmas!

Hi!

Bobby

⚜

Fuck you on Hanukkah!

Hi!

Bobby

SPECIFIC

To Dr. Laura Schlesinger:

Fuck You in particular on Hanukkah!

છ૪૪

To Ken on his new apartment!

Love you despite your personality, your looks, and your Apartment!

Warmly,

Bobby

Tom.

To a true whore,

In every sense of the word

Love,

Bobby

CRVO

Chris, sweetie!

You and Courtney Love have the same
hair stylist and bail bondsman!

Yours, and Up Yours, Bobby

To my partner, Barbara:

On Common-Law Day,

With affection,

Rebecca

⚬⚬⚬

To Betty:

Congrats on finally getting custody of your children!

Sincerely,

Allison

To Tonya:

All is forgiven!

Sorry about that Restraining Order!

Michaela

ભୂ

To Tom:

Get well!

Get out of that hospital soon.

The police are still looking, they say.

Tenderly,

Fred

BIRTHDAYS

Ken,

You don't look a day over fifty!

Happy thirtieth birthday!

Bobby

○○

Happy birthday, bitch!

I'm your bitch too!

Lovingly,

Bobby

Marge,

Hello Birthday Girl!

Oops! I mean Birthday Woman!

Yours,

Theodore

൬൳

To President Mugabe of Zimbabwe:

Birthdays come but once a year.

And so do you, alas, I hear.

But spare us the details of your love life!

YACHTING

A yacht, even a small one, can be the setting for an informal luncheon, dinner, or cocktail party, either at dockside, anchored off- shore, or moored in a deserted cove. On very hot summer days it is cooler on the water than ashore, usually with a most pleasant breeze. You can also invite friends on an All-Day Cruise with picnic lunch and interludes of fishing, swimming, and underwater exploration (although a cruise that takes an entire day can be very wearing on your guests as well as on your ego).

For refreshments keep in mind the danger of spoilage during warm weather. Thus you should serve only items full of preservatives, or consider having the affair catered piping hot by Colonel Sanders.

If you fix things yourself, you will wish to prepare plenty of cream dishes, salads made with mayonnaise, plus tapiocas and creamy desserts. Even the real sailors amongst your guests won't mind getting seasick, as it will give them a chance to brag that they have done something with the upper classes. Besides, seasickness is one of life's more human experiences and should not be missed. (Give Dramamine and such only to the sissies in the crowd.) A good purge not only cleanses the soul and the body, it feeds the creatures of the deep.

If you are a guest, the actual sailing may take you to far-off ports, where you can buy exotic items that sell for *much* more at Woolworth's back home.

Quarters may be cramped, even on the larger yachts, and you may bump your head and scrape your knees, so try being one of those with "lowered" expectations or stay confined to your bunk.

Your bunk will probably convert into something else, like a stove. Should you catch on fire during the night, douse yourself with seawater quietly, so as not to wake the others, who are just inches from where you are, and then go back to sleep.

There will be a "head" on the yacht (an unfortunate name). Under no circumstances are you to *give* any head, unless specifically requested to by the coxswain.

Don't tarry in this invariably foul-smelling cubicle, as others may be waiting – for it or for the coxswain.

When all the doors and drawers fly open while you are in the "galley" and you begin to cry because you want your mommy, don't – as this reflects badly on your host, and he or she may have the crew toss you overboard.

If you attempt to write a letter and are thrown to the ground by a sudden squall, remember that Herman Melville started out this way.

Actually, yachting may prove a bore to some, and if this should prove true for you after you have purchased your vessel, don't let it bother you. You may mask your disappointment in knowing that you are fantastically *rich*. While that of course does not guarantee happiness, it will simply have to do.

 # THE HELP

~ getting by with just one cleaning lad

It is one of the little ironies of life that today, when more people than ever before have the means, the time, and the urge to entertain, it has become practically impossible to find slaves to cope with the extra work that entertaining inevitably entails. (Naturally, we mean legal slaves, not illegal ones.)

The competent, compliant all-around slave is, alas, as extinct as the Dodo. Americans have had to struggle with this problem for some years now. Of course such labor-saving devices as the dishwasher, the microwave, the electric can opener, the automatic vegetable peeler, the blender, the infrared grille, the ice cream maker, the egg slicer, and the garlic press are useful. Still, nothing can quite replace a real-life, hard-working, live-in slave.

Freeing the slaves is just another part of all this rampant permissiveness that has been going on for some time now. Free the slaves! Stop stoning adulterous wives! Let homosexuals vote! One can only wonder where it will all end.

About the only place you can secure slaves these days is by looking in those rather sleazy advertisements in those "underground" publications, but even these usually prove unsatisfactory, as they are often covered with Crisco and want to have sex with you instead of setting your table.

Probably the most one can hope for anymore is a servant, and even those are next to impossible to find (without an accent), and many of them really seem to think that they are as good as we are! It's enough to make one weep with frustration.

Below, nevertheless, are suggestions for dealing with the help, if and when you have any —

1. Consider them as human beings until such time as they prove otherwise, and pretend to be interested in their problems, without yawning.

2. Never ask them to do anything that you would not be willing to do yourself, such as have sex with you.

3. Never ask them to do anything that you are incapable of doing yourself, such as killing squid.

4. Give them the same food and the same degree of comfort that you yourself enjoy, without, naturally, letting them eat at the same table with you or sleep in your bed. (Always go to *their* room.)

5. Insist that they be neat and well groomed. (They must wear a hairnet when cleaning or using the pool or when serving *hors d'oeuvre* to company.)

6. Have them checked for VD and ringworm in a collective examination by the family physician at least once every six weeks.

7. Pay their Social Security taxes but not the minimum wage.

8. You should not be expected to support their relatives, nor they yours.

9. They may not commit acts of gross indecency in the parlor without your permission (or your participation).

10. They should always address you with respect. After all, you *bought* them.

 # HEALTH: PART TWO

~ mental shrinkage

TREATMENT

Now you may think you are happy being gay, but of course you're not. Therefore, you will want to find a good, old-fashioned psychiatrist who will alter your orientation. Gay people are unusually lucky in the vast number of therapists still around, both here and abroad, who are more than eager to bend over backwards to help straighten them out. If the truth be told, more doctors want to change homosexuals into heterosexuals (because there aren't enough?) than the other way around – just another example of the 'special treatment' that homosexuals are forever demanding.

How fortunate that a Famous Psychiatrist has given us permission to reprint his well-known psychic guide pamphlet. Once you read this, you may decide to go to the good doctor's clinic and get the full treatment.

EVERYTHING YOU EVER WANTED TO KNOW FROM A TO K

1. Homosexuality is a sickness. Therefore, homos should be:

  a. insulted

  b. punched out

  c. flogged

2. My homo patients suffer from depression because they are:

  a. garbage

  b. lower than shit

  c. my patients

3. My treatment has done more good for homos than:

  a. exorcism

  b. leeches

  c. concentration camps

4. I have cured many homos by:

    a. berating them

    b. making them vomit

    c. berating them, then making them vomit

5. My psychotherapy has greatly contributed to:

    a. uniformity in people

    b. suicide

    c. my bank account

6. It is manly to:

    a. fuck women (up one side and down the other)

    b. start wars

    c. kill some faggot who looks at you

7. The only mature sexuality is:

    a. my kind

8. Homosexuality is caused by:

    a. close-binding mothers

    b. weak or absent fathers

    c. the evil eye

    d. all of these

9. My scientific method is the greatest thing since:

    a. bleeding

    b. voodoo

    c. lobotomies

10. If homosexuals don't take my treatment, I will:

    a. commit them to an insane asylum

    b. castrate them

    c. stamp my foot and hold my breath

(In case you are wondering, all the answers are correct.)

CORRESPONDENCE; PART TWO

~ proper form in writing

We cannot stress enough the importance of proper letters. Good penmanship is not the requirement that it used to be, but clarity (and sincerity) never go out of date. Here are some samples of acceptable missives. If you model yours on these, you will never be one of that growing crowd of the post-literate.

Always pay attention to grammar, punctuation, tone, and niceness of phrase.

Need we add — change the names from the generic ones below.

TO BE PINNED ON A BULLETIN BOARD

Dear Jack (?)

You probably don't remember me, but we had sex in the back room here last Tuesday. I don't know how to tell you this, but you have been exposed to infantile paralysis. (I never eat sugar, even in cubes, you see.) Although I don't know how to get in touch with you directly, I thought you might see this note and go to a clinic right away. I hope it is not too late.

P.S. I think you may have borrowed my wallet when we were getting to know each other. Please return the credit cards and the I.D to the clerk at the front desk. No questions asked. Keep the cash.

Thanks,

Kevin

TO AN EX-LOVER

Dear John,

How can I tell you? I have fallen in love with someone else. Hope you will understand. Don't mean to HURT you, because we did have some fun times together. Nevertheless, I believe it is time we ended Our Relationship. I knew something had started to go wrong between us when you started confiding in my mother instead of in me. I realize we've been through a lot as a couple (unemployment insurance, your anal fistula, the Advocate Experience, and your mother). But now I need my Own Space and you probably need yours.

Besides, Sabu and I are very much in love. He is an attorney, or will be, just as soon as he gets out of college, goes to law school, and passes the Bar Exam. Sabu is a great deal of fun, unlike some people I could name.

*(But I won't, since I feel the need to Remain Positive and this is no time for **Recriminations**.)*

Still love you of course, just never want to see you again. I trust you will understand. Sabu has moved into the apartment and your things are in the hallway downstairs, waiting for you when you get off work today.

Please don't make this any harder than it already is by trying to call or come up to visit. It's Over. It's been Over for a long time now. (Please don't take the Restraining Order that personally.)

May I keep your stereo as a memento of what we once had?

Regards to you mom,

Lovingly,

Martin

A LETTER OF PASSION

Dear Rex,

I have missed you more than I can say! Although it has been just seven nights since I held you in my arms, I wanted to write and tell you how much I care. First of all, I can't begin to tell you what your genitals have meant to me. Your testicles are like two robin's eggs wrapped in soft, white leather. Your penis is like an expandable telescope with which I can truly see the world for the first time. Your butt, one of Nature's marvels, is as glorious to me as the Continental Divide – and I, your pioneer!

What can I say about your nipples, except that they are so beautiful I wish you had four instead of two. Even six. I never knew what love could be until I felt your delectable organ gushing its precious fluid, like some Arabian oil well surrendering its wealth in the middle of a hot desert (and in pre-tax dollars). Everything about you, in fact, is perfect.

*Nobody has eyelids quite like yours. You also have the skin of a young Valentino and the lips of a mature Colin Farrell, not to mention the sensitivity of a Claude Jarman, Jr., in **The Yearling** (starring Gregory*

*Peck and Jane Wyman, MGM, 1946 or the bee-stung pout of Macaulay Culkin in **Home Alone**, 1990).*

If there is one thing wrong with you, it is only this — that you did infest me with some tiny vermin in my nether regions, my sweet.

Love,

Maury,

A LETTER OF RESIGNATION

Vladimir ("Butch") Putin
Supreme Commander-in-Chief
of the Armed Forces of the
Russian Federation
Stalin Air Force Base
Cold Tushski, Russia

Dear Supremeness,

I am offering this letter of resignation from the Russian Air Force (at your request) because, after eight years of service to my country, I feel it is time to try unemployment. Our little talk together has convinced me that you are probably right – I would be unable to continue to fly an airplane, as I have for the past seven years, now that my homosexuality has been revealed and I child might hear about it.

I want to take this opportunity to thank Spec 4 Breznev for bringing my sexual orientation to the attention of the military authorities. I am pleased that he is receiving an honorable discharge in exchange for providing you with this information. While my own discharge may cause some problems in the future, I am certainly grateful that you didn't put me in front of that firing squad, as first discussed, the way they do in unenlightened countries. Thank God I live in the good old U.S.S.R. (I mean the blessed Russian Federation.)

I am sorry that I will miss the court-martial you had planned, as it would have been fun to meet some of my old acquaintances (who were scheduled to testify) and experience first hand those things I have only read about, namely, justice, due process, and equal rights.

I wish you continued success in defending our beloved nation, and I was sorry to hear that you are having difficulty recruiting enough personnel to maintain the level of forces the military would like.

God Bless the Kremlin!

Captain Fedor A. Alexandrov

BEING VELL-INFORNED: PART TWO

Knowledge is different from intelligence, as we all know, but if you are deficient in the latter category, there is only so much one can do to rectify the situation. You can, however, make up for lack of brains by being invariable *au courant*. Take the following test to find out whether you are fit for the company that most LGBT people frequent.

Remember, as in all things to do with sex, only one answer is correct.

LGBT INTELLIGENCE TEST

1. Which one is likely to be more witty?

    a. a retarded parakeet

    b. a male heterosexual teenager

Answer: (a)

2. The Mormon Osmond Family was closest to:

    a. good, clean entertainment

    b. the population explosion

    c. the Hitler Youth Movement

Answer: (probably b)

3. Which one is the more likely to be male-dominated?

    a. genuine lesbian erotica

    b. Iran

    c. the National League

Answer: (not a)

4. Which person does not belong in this group of famous homosexuals?

    a. Leonardo DaVinci

    b. Leonard Matlovich

    c. Barbara Gittings

    d. Tom Cruise

    e. none of the above

Answer: (e?)

5. Lesbians most need:

    a. equal pay for equal work

    b. tokenism

    c. assertiveness training

    d. a night with Judge Judy

Answer: (a)

6. Which of these is not a well-known bisexual?

   a. Kate Millet

   b. Marlene Dietrich

   c. the Rev. Billy Graham

   Answer: (c?)

7. If you prefer uncut men, you should be careful to avoid:

   a. smegma

   b. giving hickeys on the foreskin

   c. Jews

   d. the Rev. Billy Graham

   Answer: (a, b, c. and d)

8. "Togetherness" means the same as:

   a. sharing your body lice with your lover

   b. loving your reflection in the mirror

   c. neither of these

   Answer: (c)

9. Which one does not fit?

    a. male chauvinism

    b. female chauvinism

    c. transgender chauvinism

    d. a two-by-four dildo

    Answer: (a, b, c, and d)

10. *Bondage* is to *love* as the military draft is to:

    a. boot camp

    b. prison sex

    Answer: (both?)

11. The Government gives churches that deny rights to gays:

    a. seventy-four lashes

    b. a piece of its mind

    c. tax-exempt status

    Answer: (c)

12. Sodomy is to a crime as the Catholic Church is to:

    a. goodness

    b. sanity

    Answer: (a and b)

13. Complete the sequence: 3" / 7" / 9 1/2" –

    a. infinity

    b. Bingo!

Answer: (b)

14. Complete the sequence: 1 plus 1 plus 8 by 2 equals

    a. 69

    b. 18

Answer: (a)

15. Gay Jews do not hold:

    a. up gay churches

    b. out on the Sabbath

    c. circle jerks with Hamas

Answer: (c)

16. Homosexuals want nothing more than to:

    a. make everybody that way

    b. suck off pot-bellied, ugly married men

    c. the same rights that others have

Answer: (c)

 # SMOKING

~ not endorsed by the tobacco industry

1. The only good smoker is a dead smoker.

2. Smoke rings went out with Geronimo.

3. You look *marvellous* in your oxygen tank.

4. Lesbians who smoke cigarillos are latent hetero-sexuals.

5. One *can* be a diesel and not smoke.

6. More people have contracted the heartbreak of halitosis from smoking than from sucking dick.

7. Matches were intended for arsonists.

8. Sir Walter Raleigh *should* have been beheaded.

9. Nicotine stains clash with clean fingers and intelligence.

10. Cuban cigars are part of the Communist conspiracy.

11. Yes, yes, we know you used to smoke. Trust us, your fingernails will grow back.

12. Ashtrays shouldn't be left out where pre-pubescents can see them.

13. Butts are acceptable only on pork and cute guys.

14. Some of my best friends aren't smokers.

15. Smoking should be allowed in prisons.

16. How do you think you'd feel if others blew fresh air in *your* face?

17. The Huddled Masses referred to on the Statue of Liberty do not mean the smokers gathered outside public buildings.

18. Wouldn't you know it! *Leviticus* allows smoking.

19. If you must smoke, do it in bed.

TRAVEL TIPS

~ the young person traveling alone

Without gay people, the airlines and travel agencies would go belly up. For gay people indeed like to travel, and travel they do. If you need any proof of how much, just think for a moment – how many gays do you know who are still living in the same place they were two years ago? How many are actually home when you call?! Where *are* they? They're off traveling, that's where. (Or at least moving.)

If one is to get the most out of one's adventures, the gay traveller must pay attention to etiquette in far-away places. Even little things are important. For instance, nude sunbathing in Iceland is done only in the summer months, and in England it is bad form to proposition a member of the royal family – unless he or she makes the initial overture, such as a nod of the head.

If you find yourself outside the Western Hemisphere, pay heed to the way people do things in those regions of the world, and then you will never embarrass yourself. Find yourself among a tribe of cannibals, and all you need to do is explain that you are a vegetarian, and they will find you something to eat, such as a vegan.

Remember, heathen homes are homes too, and it does no good for the image of gays for them to be seen snickering at the religious artifacts of others. How would you feel if people snickered at the Holy Bible, after all it's meant for homosexuals!? Never forget that just because a home may not have the benefit of Judeo-Christian tradition, it doesn't mean it's all bad.

Also keep in mind that if you have sex with heathens, use the missionary position. They expect it.

Keep your travel wardrobe simple. Many gay men have journeyed all over the world with only a change of underwear and a change of partner here and there. (Don't forget the Kwell.)

The young gay person, in particular, when traveling alone must be careful if he or she stays in a hostel or student dormitory. It is necessary to sleep with one's *jewels* under the pillow, or they might be lifted during the night. Of course if placing them under a pillow proves awkward, or you don't mind having your jewels lifted during the night, keep them out where all and sundry may admire and touch them. (The lesbian young person may wish to check roving hands first.)

If you plan to smuggle, don't travel by yourself, as you will need someone to telephone your folks to let them know which foreign prison you're in. Turkish jails are reported to be best for short, rather than long, stays.

Pornographic playing cards should be left behind when visiting Islamist theocracies, since the human figure is not considered a fit subject for art, however much you delight in Colt Studio's productions.

Postal cards should detail the personal highlights of your trip, but not to the point where the postal authorities seize the material.

Enjoy the beauties that you find around you. Watch the sunset, but also watch your wallet! That handsome young man who greets you so warmly in the city square no doubt really wants to give you the pleasure of his company, yet he may want an American passport even more, if only as a souvenir of your time together. Remember, it is embarrassing to have to go to the U.S. embassy and explain that your passport was stolen by a young man to whom you graciously had consented to give English lessons.

It is easier to make contacts in a foreign land if you speak at least a little of the language. Failing that, arrows pointing to your orifices often suffice.

A smile is never out of place anywhere in the world. A cheery tone of voice can work wonders, for courtesy (among other things) is contagious.

Most hotels take travelers' checks. Most hustlers take travelers' checks as well. (So keep them locked up in the hotel's safe when you entertain.)

Sexual practices in other cultures may seem disconcerting at times, but if you find that the natives do not wish to fist-fuck, you should not press the issue. Merely chalk it up to their backward ways.

You may find that some foreigners do not like to use their mouths during sex. Do not make a fuss and report them to Amnesty International. Just make your tip shorter than usual.

It is often assumed in Latin, Middle Eastern, and similar areas that the "male" is dominant and "active," whereas the "female" is "submissive" and "passive." A lecture series on stifling role-playing may be too much, especially if you don't know the language, but if you playmate treats you like scum because he's the "male" and you're the "female," the correct thing to do is squeeze the hell out of his cock with your sphincter until he passes out.

Do not take movies, videos, or photographs of the sights you've seen, since your friends and relatives should be spared pictures of *pissoirs*. Gifts brought back for friends should be expensive, or at least gaudy.

Try not to look smug as you insist on presenting your slide shows for all those of your acquaintance.

PROPER SPEECH: PART THREE

~ handling rude heterosexuals
(there they go again!)

Unpleasantness sometimes arises when words with the wrong associations are used by our straight friends. Naturally, homosexuals understand how such terms can unwittingly slip into conversation, being as sensitive as they are and realizing that frequency does have a way of facilitating usage. Total immersion, after all, has been the custom for so long. But perhaps our straight friends would less often fall into unfortunate homophobic verbal habits if they were apprised of the way that homosexuals use certain common words. Therefore, I have a drawn up a mini-lexicon of —

TERMS, STRAIGHTS SHOULD UNDERSTAND AND USE CORRECTLY

1. *pansy* — a flower of various hues notable for its sweet, almost-human face

2. *faggot* — a twig that is burned up

3. *queer* — a term for a member of a sexual minority, used only by members of the group; similar to "nigger" and "kike"

4. *cocksucker* — an all-day rooster on a stick; one meaning only

5. *misfit* — one who fits misses together; not to be confused with ms.fit, one who fits several ms. together

6. *nervous nelly* — name for a cow off her Valium

7. *bugger* — one who has intercourse with insects
   Let us go even further and suggest some whole new terms for our straight friends to use for homosexuals. (Of course in our more enlightened times, no one uses offensive terms anymore.) But just in case —

NEW TERMS

8. *instead* of pansy — *nasturtium*, as in "He's nothing but a fuckin' nasturtium!"

9. *instead of fruit* — *kiwi*, as in "All practicing kiwi must be forbidden to marry."

10. *instead of cocksucker* — *penis valet*, as in "I don't know how us guys here in San Quentin could get along without them penis valets we got here."

11. *instead of queer — unusual,* as in Tyrone, Pedro, Cedric, and Miguel are a gang of unusual bashers. (You may use *queer* to reclaim the word, but only in academic writing of the most abstruse meaning.)

12. *instead of faggot — Presto-Log,* as in "Say, I heard that Jerry's a Presto-Log!"

13. *instead of homo — human being,* as in "I liked Sal until I heard that he's a human being."

 COURTESY

~ *(and God knows what else) is contagious*

Rudeness in sex is inexcusable, but we all have times when we may not be interested in someone who is interested in us. Despite the perception among the masses that gay men will have sex with anyone, actually there is quite a bit of pickiness, as the cognoscenti well know.

POLITE REFUSALS

AT PARTIES:

1. "I'd love to, but I came with the Archbishop."

2. "I'd love to, but my lover and I are trying monotony – I mean, monogamy."

AT BARS:

1. "No thanks, I just come here to drink before the AA meeting."

2. "Thanks, no. I just come here to sit and drink alone."

3. "You look very attractive in your Royal Mounted Police uniform, but I've never been into Nelson Eddy."

4. "I somehow doubt your jihadi outfit is the genuine article. And even if it is, no."

1. "I'm just resting. (Considered more acceptable than "Fuck off, sag-ass!")

2. "I just came for the fourth time tonight." (Probably a little white lie, but it won't hurt anyone.)

3. "I'm waiting for somebody better, creep!" (Permissible only in NYC.)

INVITATIONS IN THE BATHS:

1. Slurping the lips in the corridors is not done in the better circles.

2. Leaving your door open is fine. You should close it, however, sometime before you reach thirteen visitors, as this is considered an unlucky number.

INVITATIONS AT PARTIES:

1. Unzipping your pants and pointing may be in questionable taste, as is applying dip to your tip.

2. Giving out Take-A-Number tickets, as in a delicatessen, is always gauche.

3. Do not undress and dance naked on the ice sculpture unless explicitly asked to by the host, or if you are on the *Titanic*.

IN THE SUBWAY

1. If one is punctilious, he does not trick with a guard in uniform . . . Between 2 and 2:05 P.M. . . . on Tuesdays . . . during Advent.

2. Do not proposition the driver underground, unless he signals you to with semaphores.

 # ADDRESSING ROYALTY

~ *who does she think she is?*

When attending the drag affair of your choice, you must be careful to maintain the *proprieties*. The world is in bad enough shape already without you contributing to a further decline in values. Hence:

When in the presence of Drag Royalty, wait until one is addressed. One should volunteer no remarks oneself. Needless to say, whistling with the fingers is barbaric, howsoever delectable the selection of drag queens.

Further, in speaking to queens of drag one does not use the simple expression "you." Instead, express oneself thus: "Has your Royal Highness had much lately?" (Remember, this is a tender subject, as drag and actual sex do not always easily co-exist. Never, never ask who drag queens actually get it on with, since the answers invariably produce tears.)

When presented to royalty, a gay man is expected to bow, a lesbian to curtsey. (A lesbian is also expected to refrain from lectures on Drag as Offensive to Women.)

In the presence of the Empress Herself, everyone should show a special mark of respect – gay men with heads uncovered and lesbians bowing slightly. If privileged to be introduced to the Empress, one kisses her hand, not her butt, although she may expect it.

There is so little glamour in this world, it is impolite to think that any drag queen is ugly.

If you were not elected Empress but your best friend was, remember regicide is considered tacky.

Fundamentalists should not be asked to judge drag contests, as they tend to play favorites.

Only one contestant can win the Miss Congeniality Award, although the competition will be fierce.

If you are confused about drag queens versus transvestites versus transsexuals, believe me *they* aren't.

 # SEX

~ *is it true what they say about rectums?*

Now it is likely that at some point you will get into a discussion with someone who will maintain that gays are sick. This person may even have statistics in hand. Therefore, you must be prepared to do scientific battle. Do not hesitate to grind your opponents' arguments into dust with —

FACTS

1. Fellatio is practiced by:

> *a.* otters
>
> *b.* civet cats
>
> *c.* some gay men
>
> *d.* fallen-away lesbians
>
> *e.* reluctant housewives

Answer: c and e

2. Anal sex is practiced by:

    a. all gay men

    b. no gay men

    c. some gay men

    d. no heterosexuals

    e. reluctant housewives

Answer: d (but they're lying)

3. Stand-up sex is practiced by:

    a. stand-up comedians

    b. stand-up tragedians

    c. park cruisers

    d. Marines in latrines

    e. stand-up guys

Answers: a, b, c, d, e

OTHER FINDINGS

Among White Male Respondents the most frequent sexual technique preferred is Oral Sex (Receptor), which surprised researchers.

Among Black Male Respondents the most frequent sexual technique Preferred is Oral Sex (Receptor), which amazed researchers.

(Duh.)

Among Mixed Race Male Respondents results were similar.

Manual-Genital Contact was found to be common among Hermits, while Body Rubbing was common among Lower Status Males.

The frequency with which males of all races performed Coitus Interruptus with an Orange was striking. Anal-Navel contacts among Juvenile Delinquents with Incomes under $20,000 per year held steady with findings from previous studies (27.4%) Nocturnal Emissions in Cloistered Seminaries were found to be widespread, though under-reported. Furtive Whispering to Asexuals in Public Places seemed to be growing in incidence. (3.9 % of all groups surveyed.)

Most subjects rated their sex life as either Poor, Fair, Good, Excellent or Questioning.

Gay Males (Black, White, and Mixed Race) admitted that they had had no Oral-Oral contacts with Black-Toothed Heterosexuals (or at least few repetitions).

All respondents said that some of their best friends are Sexual Dysfunctionals.

On a personal note, I have found that, although they are referred to dismissively by large swaths of common folk, cocksuckers are often very nice people.

 BAR TIPS

~ tave rns and protocols

So that you will be a social success in any taverns that you may visit we have found it imperative to **URGE** the following —

Direct eye contact with another human being is considered unnatural.

If you are a gay woman who would like to have fun without loud music, alcohol, or snooker, may we suggest that you join a lesbian convent, if that isn't redundant.

To the man cruising alone who wants to know how to get picked up in five seconds flat, we suggest dressing *exactly* like the Pope. If you would like someone warm to talk to, tip the damn bar-tender extravagantly.

Fornicating with the pinball machine is a sign of impatience.

Playing with yourself in a bar gives the wrong impression.

One does not tip a trick.

It amounts to the same thing if you think about it, but giving a potential partner a check for fifty dollars over dinner is not quite the same as giving flowers or candy earlier.

Drunks don't do it better.

Although dancing by oneself is permissible (if you're brave enough), hula dancing in back rooms is frowned upon.

You may *not* bring your sex doll to a bar as a dancing partner!

Cruising builds self-control, if not self-esteem.

And most of all, do remember that it's easier to pick up really homely people.

🎭 CHANGING CUSTOMS

The Women's Movement has brought sexism to the attention of all. Lest you commit faux pas, you must pass the following quiz. A score of four (4) or more means that you are a sexist and will be sent a complimentary copy of all issues of *Ms. Magazine*.

HOW TO TELL IF YOU ARE A SEXIST

1. Susan B. Anthony:

    a. worked for women's rights

    b. had nice legs

    c. made a mean chowder

2. The Ayatollah Khomeini of Iran:

    a. was a misogynist five times a day

    b. made the trains run on time

3. A man who cleans house is:

    a. liberated

    b. pussy-whipped

4. A man who baby sits is:

   a. doing his share

   b. probably a child molester

Answers: 1(b); 2 (b); 3 (b); 4 (b)

HOW TO TELL IF YOU ARE NOT A SEXIST

1. Pussy is:

   a. something fluffy

   b. something to be eaten out with relish

2. A woman's place is:

   a. in the kitchen

   b. by her man

   c. on top

3. Brigham Young:

   a. was a great religious leader

   b. should have helped with the dishes

Answers: 1 (a or b); 2 (c); 3 (b)

 # FOOD

~ you are what you eat

From time to time you may find it necessary to eat. If you are gay, you will wish to eat gay food. (Excuse me, make that lesbian, bisexual, transgender and gay food.) Note the many kinds available —

GREEK

Chicken Tailbones, with grapes

S&M

Bangers

Bagels and Locks

For dessert – Tough Cookies

ITALIAN

Head Cheese and Garlic

(lots of it)

IRISH

Communion Wafers,

washed down with Holy Water

and Alcohol

CLOSET

Milk Toast

MEXICAN

Bloody Maricones

CALIFORNIACUISINE

Capers

SPECIAL DISHES

Eggs Marine (over easy)

Trannie Turnovers

Deep Dish Dyke Pie

Nor should we forget the other kind of food, often served to gays by straight people.

STRAIGHT FOOD

ARMY

Warmed-Over Tripe

JEWISH

Kosher Manna from Heaven

FUNDAMENTALIST

Nuts

SOUTHERN

Crackers

CHINESE

Small portions

Family Style Only

AMERICAN

Baloney on White Bread

(with preservatives),

served with lumpy mashed potatoes, grease gravy, and more baloney

HEALTH: PART THREE

~ getting it together

How's your health? Could be better? Very few of us are in top- notch shape. We don't eat right; we don't get enough sleep; we abuse our bodies.

Well, sometimes our bodies begin to tell us "Enough is enough now!" The wise person does not wait until that happens. He/She takes care of that marvelous vessel before it is too late.

Herewith follows a true-false test to enable you to check up on yourself, get in shape, and stay there —

TRUE / FALSE TEST

1. You can overdoes on yogurt

Answer: True

2. The quickest way to achieve weight loss is death.

Answer: True

3. You don't have to be over twenty-one to join Amyl Anonymous.

Answer: True

4. Fist-fucking, if it still exists, shows a commitment to human exploration similar in spirit, if not in scope, to the travels of Marco Polo.

Answer: True

5. Fisting is often a welcome relief from the wasteland of television.

Answer: True

6. More than one fist per rectum is unnatural and uncalled for.

Answer: True

7. Too much wrinkle cream makes you attractive to pedophiles.

Answer: Too True

8. One gallon of sperm has fewer calories than one smile from a game-show host.

Answer: True

9. Vitamin deficiencies are usually caused by eating vegetarians.

Answer: True

10. A night at the baths has more protein value than 715 Big Macs.

Answer: True

11. Running for an hour a day makes you a blow-hard.

Answer: True

12. Running for sheriff in Mississippi tightens the sphincter.

Answer: True

13. One leafy green vegetable per day will keep you from having a voice like Truman Capote's.

Answer: True

14. Vigorous sexual activity is better than deep breathing over the telephone.

Answer: True

Note: Reading Material

Forty Sordid Things to Do with Soybeans

Eat My Meat: The Butcher's Manual

PRISON PROTOCOL

~ "Mr. Jones, may I present Mr. Smith?"

Should you ever have occasion to find yourself in prison, be aware that there are Very Definite Rules of Behavior, rules that you violate only at some Very Real Peril to an agreeable social life there. Please heed the following:

The other inmates may at first seem to have snarls on their faces and growls upon their lips, but do not be misled by superficial appearances. If you are reasonably healthy and have kept yourself presentable, you can be assured of a warm and enthusiastic welcome. Hospitality toward new prisoners has long been a hallmark of most prison systems.

The formalities have been streamlined in recent years. The basic principle is always to present the less important person to the more important, the younger to the older. The most Frequent Phrases are these:

"Mr. Jones, may I present Mr. Smith?"

"Mr. Jones, I don't believe that you have met Mr. Smith."

"Mr. Jones, Mr. Smith has asked me to introduce him to you."

(Do not use "Mr. Jones" and "Mr. Smith" if the inmates happen to have different names.)

Feel free to call others by their first names, such as "Bubba," "Spike," or "Mad Dog," but only after you have been formally introduced first.

Very likely you will be invited to a private party by the other inmates as soon as you arrive. On the way to the party, they may want to show you various parts of the facilities and may actually accompany you in a group. You are advised to insist on having a guard act as chaperone in such situations, as it is not — I repeat not — fitting for a newcomer to be fraternizing with men that he barely knows. One's reputation could be damaged irreparably.

If you are lonely, something is decidedly wrong. From all reports, it is amazingly easy to be on intimate terms with the "gang" in no time at all.

However, it is usually expected that, soon after you settle in, you will choose an associate in whom you can confide, a trusted confidant, as it were. He is affectionately known as your "daddy," and you are affectionately known as his "punk." He will take care of all those little annoyances that might come your way, such as unwanted kisses thrown by the other inmates and surprise pajama parties held in the shower when you least expect them. You, in turn, will provide housekeeping service and ass. (It makes for a very tidy arrangement all around and has been the Moral Bedrock upon which even outside civilization rests.) It's probably best if you convince yourself it's consensual, sort of like wives in countries with arranged marriages.

If you have any problems, be sure to seek the assistance and counsel of a guard or other member of the staff, perhaps even the concierge, for they are more than willing to see that you are enjoying your stay, and of course you should "tip" them for any extra services or courtesies rendered.

Don't forget to sign up for the Frequent Stays Program. Some lovely gifts are available through this program, including lawyer referrals and AIDS medications.

If you are known to be homosexual, the authorities will go out of their way to make your visit a special delight, greeting you daily with warm nicknames and even croissants and other evidence of their joy that you are residing in the facility. It should give you a glow to know that you are singled out for particular notice.

It is considered impolite to leave prison before the time your host has set for guests. That is why there is a very specific time on your invitation.

If at any time you should see any persons being mistreated, you will of course notify an agent of the state or federal government so that the abuse can be remedied immediately, as it undoubtedly will be.

If you are allowed conjugal visits, whatever you do, don't ejaculate prematurely, as this tends to make your visitor feel that he has driven a long way for very little, however splendid your conversation may be.

When you leave prison, do not be remiss – a thank-you note is always expected.

OUR STRAIGHT FRIENDS

~ *that majority in our midst*

Some of my best friends are heterosexuals. Believe it or not, some people of this persuasion can actually be pleasant to be around.

True, some of them do tend to be flamboyant and flaunt themselves by holding hands and smooching on the street, and often tend to be accompanied by the consequences of their actions (children), but we must learn to overlook these faults because so many of them really are quite talented. A few have even contributed to civilization. I believe it was a heterosexual who invented the prophylactic.

If given half a chance, they are quite sensitive and have been known to make such pretty trinkets out of lumber and cement. I saw one once who was an orderly in a hospital, and a very fine job he did of it too!

Oh yes, heterosexuals can be especially delightful dinner guests, not to mention useful for filling in that extra place when you have a last-minute cancellation. You may not want to live next door to one, naturally, or have the males teaching little girls in the lower grades, but if you keep an open mind you may find out just how sweet they can be. So stop being negative and give hets a break.

To help you overcome any prejudice, we have prepared a list to learn by heart and to use when appropriate.

POSITIVE THINGS TO SAY ABOUT HETEROSEXUALS

1. They don't:

> — see *The Women* seventeen times

> — wear boots to bed

> — give lubricants as presents

2. They never:

> — give up hope that their children will marry

> — stop cruising even in their eighties

> — kill for opera tickets

> — meet their spouses in back rooms

3. Heterosexuals *wash* their jock straps.

 # PUNISHMENTS

~ discipline

If you are the parent or guardian of a gay child, no doubt he or she will be an angel 99% of the time. Once in a while, however, even the gay child can be naughty.

Here follow some appropriate punishments —

FOR BAD GAY BOYS

1. No poppers for a week

2. Stay in their room and read Gordon Merrick for two whole days

3. Stay indoors and play with themselves (Excuse me – play *by* themselves)

4. Take away their suntan lotion

5. Make them surrender their Bette Midler tickets (And no Cher farewell tour, not even one!)

6. Gooey desserts for a solid week with no exercise allowed

7. Hide their bikini briefs

FOR BAD GAY GIRLS

1. Make them wear a dress

2. Make them look at a dildo

3. No outfielder's mitt this Christmas

4. No Melissa Ethridge tickets (or Sarah McLachan or Indigo Girls tickets)

5. No male bashing for an hour and a half

6. Give them an *In*significant Other

7. No golden retrievers.

8. No bragging about starting the Stonewall Uprising.

READING MATERIAL

~ who's "in" and who's "out"

Now we come to literature! How our hearts swell with pride at the Gay Heritage in this realm! (A book is pieces of paper with words on them, for those who aren't sure.) Do not the names themselves inflate your gay chest – Walt Whitman, Herman Melville, Henry James, Willa Cather, Horatio Alger, Mary Renault, Gordon Merrick? On and on. And these are merely some of the past glories of our tradition. Today, now, at this very moment, new gay literature appears daily. More gay male readers are reading more books than at a any other time in history – and doing it with just one hand too! More gay women are delving into the intricate symbolism of pulp novels than you can shake a stick at.

Publishers as well are seeking nothing but the best work, and for once, in a crassly commercial world, quality is shining through! Editors in New York have been arrested for soliciting manuscripts in a public place. Writers are writing as they never have before, with integrity and correct punctuation, without bitchery or envy, and who but the cynical would not be thrilled by these developments?! (And what's more: some of this may even be read ten years from now.)

As for what the socially in-tune should read, please pay careful attention to the following —

ACCEPTABLE READING MATTER

1. Soft-Core

2. Hard-Core

3. Masturbation Books (Also called Self-Help)

4. Expensive Coffee Table Volumes (for those who can't read)

5. For your friends with high IQ's: Proust and . . . This Book

UNACCEPTABLE READING MATTER

1. *The Joy of Child Molesting*

2. *The Secret Heterosexual Life of Truman Capote*

3. St. Paul

Literature has the National Book Awards, the Pulitzers, and the Nobel Prize. Why not some gay literary prizes, beyond the Lammies, which we never win anyway. Hence our suggestions —

ANNUAL GAY LITERARY AWARDS — AND THE FIRST RECIPIENTS

1. The Bad Taste Ribbon

> —all the gay bar rags in all the gin joints in all the small towns in America

2. The Mother Theresa Compassion Award

> — to Critic John Simon

3. The Stalin Prize for Literature

> — to *The Body Politic*

4. The Oscar Wilde Wit Award

> — no prize awarded his year

5. The Thornton Wilder Closet Medallion

> — to Anonymous

6. The Tennessee Williams Let-It-All-Hang-Out Biography Button

> — to Greg Louganis

7. The Nikolai Gogol Starving Artist Cup

> — to the memoirs of Rosie O'Donnell

8. The Rod McKuen Doggerel Award

> — to too many gay-bashing rap and reggae artists to name individually

9. The Yukio Mishima Self-Publicity Award

> — to the Rev. Ted Haggard

Addendum: California has now considered, although not yet implemented, mentioning in school texts that some famous people have been gay. Hooray! But let us hasten to console those troubled by this that such information would clearly be available only to high school students, never to impressionable *grade schoolers*, who must continue to learn who's gay from the finest schoolyard lexicon, where the terms *fag* and *homo* reign supreme.

 # GIFTS

~ who's "in" and who's "out"

Everybody knows not to give sexist toys anymore, such as guns to boys and dollhouses to girls, right? And everybody knows not to give dangerous toys to anyone, such as bee bee guns. But what does one give to the Homosexual Children of Your Acquaintance, possibly without telling their parents that you know? Here are some ideas for non-sexist, safe (and out) gifts:

FOR THE GAY BOY CHILD

1. A pair of Levi's, tight

2. A codpiece (Junior size, or possibly Husky)

3. A date with a Boy Scout (Eagle Rank)

4. A near-membership in the Boy Scouts (almost equal in value to the real thing)

5. A Lone Ranger cock-ring

6. Not Gay Bob

7. A subscription to *Out* (the pre-teen edition)

8. Fruit of the Loom Pampers

9. High heels?

10. Madonna tickets

FOR THE GAY GIRL CHILD

1. A pair of Levi's, loose

2. A complete set of Sappho (child's edition)

3. A Gertie Stein Betsy Wetsy doll

4. Not a necktie

5. A k.d. laing spelling primer

6. A ticket out of Nigeria, India, or Russia, to name a few

 # CAREERS

~ who's "in" and who's "out"

Gay men love show business. Who else can tell you the middle names of all of Lana Turner's husbands plus their astrological signs?

Well, if you're thinking of making Show Biz your career, we suggest that you saturate yourself with the gossip columnists. Maybe you can even, one day, write your own gossip column. Like this —

McCauley Skulking, former child star, dismissed for having an erection during the filming of a Walt Disney movie, is said to be making a comeback in a psychological bike movie being produced by Roger Corman Productions and Yamaha Motors.

There's talk of an Oscar for porn star Cal Parker's sensitive performance in *Horny in the Morning*.

And there's no truth whatsoever, according to his manager, that Rod Longer isn't up to his Usual Standards in his latest flick and had to look at animal pornography to get it up at all.

Seen having a man-to-man talk at Ciro's (without their wives) were virile Studs Terkel and Ice Cube. (What were you talking about, fellas?)

Alas, the late Hedy Lamar, once a great film beauty, was caught dead shop-lifting in the Notions Department of Seven-Eleven in Bakersfield, California.

Recuperating at Cedars of Sodom Hospital from that awful accident with a gerbil, legendary actor Richard Gere is said to be on the road to recovery after having fifty stitches in part of his anatomy. (The gerbil was rescued by the SPCA but later had to be euthanized.)

Angela Lansbury, one of Hollywood's oldest surviving stars from its Golden Age, was visibly touched by the gift from the cast and crew of her latest film (in which she plays herself in a cameo) and said that she was going to find a good use for the three-speed vibrator they gave her.

(Supposed to be so good for those overused facial muscles.)

Tallulah Bankhead, came out of her grave last week to sue us for misquoting her in this column last month. Miss Bankhead denies that she ever said she got her last name from performing fellatio on several branches of Chase-Manhattan.

Steady As They Go – a Famous Male Homosexual and a Famous Female Homosexual. Hooray for one of Hollywood's longest-lasting marriages!

Big bucks are said to be involved in a project to bring *The Joy of Oral Sex* as a mini-series to TV with Tony Danza and several unknowns onboard.

Tuesday Bergman shocked all of Hollywood last week by giving birth to twins in wedlock!

Seen kissing the current Pope's butt at a Vatican "do" were several gay Catholic celebrities oh so grateful for a crumb. Merely because the One, Holy, Catholic, and Apostolic Church isn't burning you at the stake, it is still not your friend.

A Famous Male Star's last request was that he be buried in the same niche with his Personal Secretary of the past twenty-two years, but relatives have contested the will.

Colin Farrell, having had limited success playing Alexander the Great, has chosen to play an Irishman who swears a lot in *My F——Left Foot II*.

RIP Shirley Temple. Now *there* was a Honey Boo Boo.

Numerous men have played gay parts by now, but action star Vin Diesel is making plans to star as a lesbian truck driver in an update of *Little Women* (working title: *Big Women*).

Houses in Tinsel Town continue to be built with Very Large Closets.

Box Office Poison: *My Life with a Catholic Alcoholic*, a movie showing that Katharine Hepburn despised Spencer Tracy and he, her.

Nathan Lane has purchased Mary Pickford and Douglas Fairbanks' old Home, Pickfair, from Pia Zadora and is re-naming it Pickfairy.

We can't begin to tell how sadly the news of the death of Ramon Navarro still haunts us on its anniversary. It is reported that he died in his sleep, taken care of at the last by two youthful companions whom he had befriended and given shelter. An unconfirmed rumor has it that they were at Ramon's bedside when he passed on.

 # READING

~ *a dying custom?*

If you decide to give someone a book as a present, you must be careful to give what is suitable (even though no one will read it). What follows are two lists of right and wrong books, a sort of Gay Index.

RELIGIOUS BOOKS

1. *Ecclesiastical Drag*
   by Pope John Paul II

2. *On Gay Rights*,
   a brief paragraph by Pope Benedict XVI.

3. *My Pastor, My Lover*,
   by Sally Eaton-Pusey,
   (published by Unitarian Books)

LITERARY CRITICISM

1. *Tragic Camp in the Fiction of Susan Sontag*,
   by Mario Paz

2. *Latent Heterosexuality in the Essays of Rita Mae Brown*,
   by Lillian Faderman

3. *Aesthetic and Mimetic Rhythms in Torso Magazine Illustrations*
   by Erich Auerbach

4. *Sex Roles in Albanian Pornography*   ,
   by William Empson

5. *The Loosened Knot: Cock-Ring Imagery in Twentieth Century Male Homoerotica*
   by G. Wilson Knight

6. *Comic Dissonance in Masters and Johnson Reports*
   by Jerry Rosco

MISCELLANEOUS

1. Betty Crocker's *Homosexual Cooking*

2. *Fodor's Guide to Gay Bars in Ancient Greece*

3. *Designer Gay Babies*, by the cast of *Queer Eye*

UNACCEPTABLE

1. *A Treasury of Jerry Falwell Sermons*

2. *The Collected Hate Speeches of Fred Phelps and Hezbollah*

3. *A Concordance to Biblical Sodomy Jokes*

4. *The Wit and Wisdom of the Ayatollahs*

& *This Book*

⚜ SEX MENACE

Whether you know it or not, there is a growing menace in our midst. It's time that some of our social guardians (like me) said something about it.

A dedicated group of sexual deviates is out to impose its perversion on others. This group cannot reproduce, so it has to recruit.

We speak of noting less than the greatest threat to the family since boredom – the **Militant Celibate!** (Sometimes also known as the Obstinate Abstinent.)

That's right, militant celibates are appearing in ever-growing numbers, refusing to get wed, even to live together in sin, and expecting the rest of us to accept their unnatural ways. Well, their little game is just about up. The Secret Police (oops, we mean the FBI) have prepared a report (of which we have the only copy) detailing how they operate.

DID YOU KNOW?????

They start out in small cells, very often springing, as strange as it may sound, from quite wholesome families, and then these cells spread out in wider and wider circles until they eventually will make the whole world celibate!

They are known to hang around places where children play, and, horrible as it may sound, some of them are even *coaches*! You can imagine how they insinuate their militant unnatural celibacy into the sports instruction they give our innocent young folk.

Fortunately some of them can be detected by their odd clothes, though more and more of them are dressing in plain-clothes and thus can go undetected until it is too late. (What is the world coming to! Only the Vice Squad has the right to wear plain-clothes!)

The usual method by which these perverts get our youth is to show them pictures of people *not having sex*! Can you imagine what this does to unsuspecting minds!? One little girl in Wabash, Indiana who viewed some this celibate filth didn't have sex for the rest of her life and wound up in an institution for the mentally insane!

These perverts had been lying low for a few years, but now, once again, they have a well-coordinated plan, funded at the Highest Levels, to move into our schools and offer courses in *Non-Sex* Education! The Secret FBI Report quotes one of their leaders bragging that he would not rest until he has erased every trace of sexual knowledge from the minds of the world's youth. "When I finish with them, they won't know intercourse from a hole in the ground," he said.

They even have churches of their own! They cover their bodies with layers of uncomfortable clothes and often wear ugly hats and sing songs written especially for them. Then they take up collections, so far raising millions for their nefarious purposes. Some celibates even tithe, and the funds go into a big bank account in a foreign country. They use this money to influence legislation in their favor, even to enact laws that will make being celibate *normal*!!!

There's no telling exactly what they look like, because celibates try to pass, but rumor has it that many of them are grossly fat and ugly, all the better to entice us into celibacy.

But thank God, it's still not too late to halt this menace. If you are watchful, you can catch them and turn them over to the authorities. Some sure signs that you are dealing with celibates include these —

1. They own single beds.

2. They say no when you ask for a date.

3. If you married to one (Heaven forbid!), they always have a headache.

If you discover any, even if it's within your own family, it is your duty to expose them. If we don't root them out now, the next thing you know they will be asking for equal treatment under the law. They may even wish to be in the military. (Can you imagine what a celibate soldier would be like?!) Eventually it can lead to only one thing – making the rest of us *watch* them being celibate! Oh, my God, don't let this happen! Act now!

 # THE CENSUS

~ just how many of them are there?

Every ten years the US Government takes a census of the U.S. population, to determine how many divorced people living in designer shacks have bathrooms with French doors and other "facts." There are questions about ethnic distribution and annual income but Very Little about another subject of Some Importance to Same-Sex Devotees. Well, at long last, the Government is about to include some questions about a Hidden Population . . . just how many **Homophobes** are there in the nation?

The gay person will of course wish to know the results of this poll so that he or she will have a heads up and thus always behave in the most discreet way possible.

We have managed to gain access to this new section of the census and are only too glad to share it with you.

(Alas, we don't have the Answer Sheet.)

1. Society ought to give homosexuals:

    a. a fair shake

    b. a Rorschach test

    c. electric shock treatments

2. The worst thing about lesbians is that they:

    a. started the Black Plague

    b. stick with their own kind

    c. don't stick with their own kind

3. Someone who has never had a homosexual experience:

    a. is the norm

    b. doesn't know what they're missing

    c. is working for a faith-based Federal agency

4. There are almost no homosexuals in Red China because:

    a. the authorities say so

    b. homosexuality is a sign of bourgeois decadence

    c. honorable surveys not accurate

5. There are no homosexual Evangelical preachers because:

    a. homosexuals lisp

    b. Christ warned us against them

    c. some people believe anything

6. The world desperately needs:

    a. designer genes

    b. fewer people

    c. black conservative Alan Keyes to run again for office

7. Some think that we still should not have homosexuals in the armed services because:

   a. Alexander the Great didn't

   b. The ancient Greeks didn't

   c. they aren't as masculine as the women there

   d. lesbians may be more masculine than the generals

8. Gay pilots tend to be:

   a. flighty

   b. in and out

   c. down and dirty

9. Homosexuals would be better off if they:

   a. acted like real men

   b. acted like they did in the old days

   c. carried guns

10. Homosexuals are worse than:

   a. cancer of the prostate

   b. illegal aliens

   c. Tea Party tea parties

11. Children who have gay teachers will grow up to be:

    a. gay

    b. Japanese

    c. adults

12. The Soviets were correct to put homos in prison because:

    a. they might find a lover there

    b. they feel more comfortable with their own kind

    c. they're used to it

13. The right-wing is anti-gay because:

    a. all homos are Commies

    b. all Commies are homo

    c. all Commies eat hominy

    d. gay marriage causes cancer

    e. gay marriage will lead to polygamy in Muslim countries

MANNERS IN GENERAL

1. Faux etiquette is better than no etiquette.

2. You may picket the Archbishop of Canterbury with your Gay Lib signs whilst having High Tea with him; however, you may not leave them on the tea table, as with elbows.

3. In this world you will not like everyone, nor will everyone like you. The point is to make your friends laugh and your enemies cry.

4. However much your accent may be upper-class, it is severely compromised by the over-use of "like, you know" as spoken filler. Over-use consists of more than once per century, and please pass this down to your heirs.

5. You may make use of a castle's stationery when you visit, but you cannot put "Lord" before your name.

6. At meals, save those naughty bits about your personal hygiene failures for private conversations with the servants – or for you unpublished memoirs.

7. Remember, servants are now literate (occasionally) and can write memoirs too.

8. "Airs" are not "heirs," although pronounced the same, because the former are what you try to put on while the latter are what you try to put off.

9. True style is bred in the bone, but if you're from Hoboken you can at least occasionally try.

10. Good manners ante-date the Ten Commandments by a good ten thousand years.

11. You can still be a Strong Woman and use a deodorant.

12. Be as attractive as long as you can be. And then die.

13. Though punctilious in every other detail of proper behavior, oddly enough fundamentalists of all religious stripes tend *not* to follow this etiquette guide.

THE GAY AGENDA

1. The right of lesbian horses to marry in Connecticut!

2. For hardware stores to have a section clearly labeled LESBIAN SECTION, if not an entire separate store!

3. Place cards at Papal orgies!

4. If a gay man is beaten to a pulp at Burger King, he is entitled to a complimentary dessert!

5. A plaque at the Holocaust Museum.

6. Until gay marriage is approved everywhere, the only solution would seem to be Gay Suicide Bombers at Bloomingdale's!

7. Until Nigeria repeals its vicious anti-gay laws, Gay, Lesbian, and Questioning Suicide Bombers at the UN. (Even some UN action would be good.)

8. Until gay bashings cease, Suicide Bombings by Parents and Friends of Gays at Southern Baptist conventions everywhere.

9. Gay Pride Parades in Riyadh!

10. Shorter prison sentences in Egypt!

11. Affirmative Action in the U.S. military hierarchy! Rosie O'Donnell would clean up the Pentagon!

12. Reparations for past discrimination in the US military. Mail me a check now!

13. They say that the Affirmative Action policy for gays is coming along nicely in Iran and Saudi Arabia, until which time you may find your beheading or hanging a minor irritant.

14. Black ministers to find other parts of the Bible to raise money with!

15. Tax breaks for gay churches!

16. Fashionable attire for gay celibate monks!

17. For past discrimination a casino of my very own would be quite nice.

18. The right to say "my lover and I" anywhere, anytime without flinching!

GAY MARRIAGE TOASTS

1. "Remember, if you're fighting at least you're not lonely!"

2. "To those who criticized us for sleeping around and now can't wait to stop us from being faithful!"

3. "To all the people who will stop getting married because gays are allowed to!"

4. "To the same people who stopped voting when women got the vote!"

5. "Long life and happiness! And drink up fast before they annul this ceremony! . . . Oops! Too late."

6. "To the members of Congress who feel threatened because we may have the same piece of paper they have!"

7. "To all the millions of people who will want to marry their dogs because we are solemnizing our union today!"

8. "Next a Constitutional Amendment to prevent straight divorce — makes more sense than the Defense of Marriage Act!"

9. "I didn't really want a gay marriage, but my mother on her death bed made me promise at least to try!"

10. "May your gay marriage be equal to straight marriage, followed by gay boredom, gay spousal abuse, and gay divorce!"

✎ ONLINE DATING

1. You may lie about your age, height, sex, sexual prowess, and class origins, but if you are a mass murderer you must say so upfront.

2. Never date a terrorist online. He may be leading you on.

3. Do not give up your lease or your job to move in with a person you have only just exchanged smutty messages with.

4. You may exchange pleasantries in the first few "chats." You may not exchange bodily fluids except on your separate computers.

5. You may Talk to a Naked Girl or a Hung Hunk, but don't insist that they be a friend for life.

6. Once you have a met online, a gracious thank-you card for a charming "in-person" interchange is always thoughtful; however, a surprise video of the two of you made with your video-phone could smack of blackmail.

7. That lady spreading her thighs for your enthrallment, though no doubt sincere and nurturing, is perhaps not forever faithful.

8. Sex chat can be fun, but don't be surprised if you feel used afterward.

9. Sex chat can be very good. However, if you want to smoke afterwards, please note that's bad, bad, bad!

10. Clean the keyboard after you if you are in a public library or using government property. Thank you.

CELL PHONE

1. Cell phones should primarily be used in cells.

2. Speak softly . . . and don't be a Big Dick.

3. The individual you are calling may be deaf and far away. Those close to you in the room are not.

4. Drive and chat on your cell phone — go to jail. (Or to Hell)

5. Not everyone is interested in your use of profanity as your every other word.

6. The vast extent of your limited vocabulary need not be known to so wide a population.

7. No one looks his or her best in a car crash caused by poor cell phone etiquette.

8. If your phone is on 'vibrate' rather than on 'ring' in a public place, good for you. Still, you may not 'come' no matter how much you may be inclined.

9. People whose cell phones interrupt others' lives should be stoned to death, preferably with old cell phones, thus providing a double public service.

10. A cell phone was once used for a worthy purpose. Possibly.

11. Though exceedingly rare, cell phones and etiquette can go together.

HOW TO EAT BRITISH FOOD

1. The Hearty English Breakfast in so-called Merrie Old England at times consists of cold toast and the colder shoulder.

2. Nothing is better than scones with bed and butter.

3. Unless, that is, it is Trifle, served up by the Eastern European busboy.

4. Or maybe Spotted Dick. . . . I'll pass. (Spotted with what?!)

5. Yum! Clotted cream (Clotted with what?!)

6. Tea Without Sympathy (made with Thames water and no milk)

7. Haggis: a Scottish dish served separately from the British staff.

8. Kidney pie (with free dialysis afterward)

9. Be careful what you eat. Now, now, a pastry puff is not the same thing as a pastry pouf.

10. To be serviced by male staff always keep a stiff upper lip and a stiffy below.

11. If on the guest list, you may poach an egg on His Lordship's estate, but not game.

12. Have some toffee with your coffee and a lolly under your brolly. It is not baby-talk! You are in the (once) United Kingdom.

HOW TO HANDLE THINGS FRENCH

1. There are rude people, there are extremely rude people, and then there are the French.

2. Gallic charm is akin to Alaskan sunbathing, not unknown but rare.

3. The late Duke of Windsor lived for many years in France, but then he also was so stupid he gave up the throne of England for an American woman homely enough to be his housekeeper.

4. On the sly, French designers always shop at Costco.

5. The French do know how to cook delicious food, but they haven't a clue as to what to do about their Muslim problem.

6. Wine and nicotine stains are sexy, if you are a prisoner on Devil's Island for twenty years.

7. Charles DeGaulle had a big nose.

8. Chanel Number 5 has always out-sold Number 1 and Number 2.

9. We do not hate the French. We simply never want to see them again.

10. French children are alcoholics.

HOW TO BUY THE CORRECT CAR

1. Consider getting the Lexus "Important."

2. Avoid the Chevrolet "Impotent."

3. Do you really want a Cadillac "Pimp"?

4. Think twice before ordering that Toyota "Loser."

5. The Prius "P.C." (Is it really 4 U?)

6. The Ford "Wimp" makes a nice gift for an ex-lover.

7. The Buick "Big Shit" may be misunderstood.

8. The Ford "Fuck You," we guarantee, will be vandalized.

9. The Altima "Ass Action" comes with adjustable seats. But it has been involved in several ass-action lawsuits.

10. A Mitsubishi "STD" is asking for it.

11. The Saab "Story" and the Saab "Sissy" are out of stock, or should be.

12. Smart cars (tiny autos) are driven in Europe – but only by illegal Hobbits.

13. The Jaguar "Twit" is giving mixed signals.

14. The Infiniti "Billionaire's Penis" is the most stolen car.

15. The Kia "Child Molester" is the least stolen car.

AT THE RACES

1. Bet on Daddy's Little Bugger over Nancy Boy.

2. But Nancy Boy may surprise you in a long-distance sweepstakes, especially over Macho Fucker.

3. Prancing Stallion to Show. (You go, guy!) (Disco Stallion is lame.)

4. Disco Bunny? (Still going after all these years?)

5. Flasher (to Show, naturally)

6. Viagra's Boy in the stretch.

7. Whoa Nelly in the Camptown Races.

8. Strong Womyn to Win, Place, and Show.

9. Diesel Annie in the Kentucky Derby. (You go, girrrl!)

10. Gelding's Delite. (Yeah, sure.)

11. Lonesome Willy. (Do horses masturbate? Whom does one ask?)

12. Mare's Missionary Position. (In the Het Stakes only)

13. Filthy Filly (good mudder)

14. Lesbian Mom (good mother)

15. Sex Slave (still in the stall until told to come out)

FOR THE LADY TRAVELLER

1. Baring your face is "cool" in desert countries, and may Allah have mercy upon your soul.

2. In countries where a head covering is mandatory, do cover your head. But bare your breasts at every opportunity to disconcert the bastards.

3. The full burqa (chador) is useful, since it not only serves as clothing but can double as a tent when abandoned by your husband because you drove a car.

4. Lesbians are known to choose the veil in Islamic regions of influence.

5. Have sex with whoever you choose, but keep your passport in the hotel's safe.

6. For bisexuals in particular, no doubt he finds your smile alluring, your vagina one of a kind, but doubt the insincerity of his hard-on if he asks you to marry him in mid-orgasm, yours or his. (Especially yours.)

7. Bossy is bossy, whether you're in Boston or Beirut.

8. You are brave and independent in going to Uzbekistan alone in your bikini, no matter what your guidebook says.

9. You are courageous and self-reliant in traveling everywhere by yourself. You are not crabby and incapable of compromise! (Tell yourself that.)

10. Sharing a cabin on a cruise ship to save money is financially wise. But oh so déclassé.

11. Your partner has left you, arthritis has kicked in, and the Deutschmark is terrible against the dollar, but you got a chocolate on your pillow.

12. If you were a man and did what you did, they would not criticize you. You're correct. They would cut off your balls.

13. If you are demanding and obnoxious, they call you a bitch. If a man is demanding and obnoxious, they will call him . . . a bitch.

AT MORE RACES

1. Perky Member by a nose.

2. Get a Room. (the two of you in stalls #3 and #4)

3. Alice B. Sappho by a tongue

4. Anne Heche was a washout in the Proud Lesbian Stakes.

5. Rosie O'Donnell managed to win the Mainstream Stakes. (But stop with the kids already!)

6. Ass Muncher. (well back in the pack)

7. Lickety Split favored in several races of the AerLingus Hurdles (or something Lingus) over the general heavy favorite, Big Dickie, in the Endurance Handicap.

8. Smart Ass is the even-money favorite in the Royal Asscot.

9. Big Bottom knows how to Place.

10. Cork Sucker (for those who favor fine wines)

11. Rear Admiral (is not dirty!)

12. Citation. (Is the Vice Squad still doing this?)

13. Schlong is sure to pull one out in a photo finish.

14. Always gallop to the finish line (but not too prematurely)

TIPS FOR TRAVELLERS

1. Never travel alone (or with somebody else, either).

2. Carry your own luggage – and you can carry on all that much sooner once you get there.

3. When cruising in a country known for its gay-bashing, always leave your passport in your hotel and your stun gun in your back pocket.

4. Always pack carefully – cock on the left, balls on the right.

5. Be understanding of native customs, unless they are homophobic. Then try to change them as fast and as soon as you can. (After all, there is only so much shit one has to take in this world.)

6. Men holding hands in certain countries are not gay. (Just Questioning.) (Don't question them, though.)

7. A portable bidet (pronounced bee-day) is perfection on gay cruises.

8. A smile is understood universally, as is a blow-job.

9. The vegan sheep head's soup is said to be excellent in rural Cyprus.

10. You may be forced to resort to self-abuse in large parts of the Outback.

11. The Outback does not mean that you can be "out" at the mines.

12. The men having gay sex with you in Latin or Arabic nations aren't gay. (Just Questioning.)

TIPS WHAT YOU MUST NOT SAY ABOUT . . .

1. The Vatican and St. Peter's Basilica are great . . . if that fucking Pope would move out. (He did!)

2. Hadrian's Wall or your tour guide's penis . . . how long is it?

3. The Statue of Liberty . . . if a terrorist airplane flies up her skirts, is it statutory rape?

4. The Grand Canyon . . . you've seen bigger assholes at Republican conventions.

5. The Alaskan Wilderness . . . you and your life partner may be forced to have sex again!

6. Detroit . . . means "don't bother" in French. The plural of Detroit is "Detritus."

7. The Great Wall of China . . . wasn't it meant to keep round-eyes out?

8. The Japanese . . . at least they go home after they visit.

9. Mexico . . . hey, why don't they do some work there!

10. San Francisco . . . a myth, like chivalry, that never was, except in travel brochures and false

dreams. . . . a Third World locale notable for its large numbers of charmingly homeless drunks and drug addicts.

11. New York, New York . . . if you can make it there, maybe you have lousy ambitions.

12. London . . . is there anybody British there?

13. India . . . being gay is illegal there, because India needs more reproduction.

14. India . . . outsourcing jobs from the U.S. insures that you will get poor service and bad communication not only abroad but at home.

15. Remember – if you diddle His Holiness, wash your finger with holy water afterwards.

16. People are never stereotypes, even when they are.

17. There always seems to be a word in every era that stops honest speech. In the Dark Ages it was *heretic*. In the 1950s it was *communist*. Today the word is *racist*.

18. Come on, admit it . . . you would participate in an orgy with George W. Bush.

19. Lady Hammer says there are two things one should avoid in life at all cost: partially hydrogenated oils and Dodi Fayed.

🐓 MORE TRAVELLING

1. That charming fellow who turns out to be a hustler should be soundly whipped, and for free!

2. One rim job in Jakarta is a lark. Two show a blatant disregard for the goals of the World Health Organization.

3. If you must finger that fox in Outer Mongolia, please ablute by the time you reach Inner Mongolia.

4. One helping of cum at a time. Two or more may make your glands swell.

5. Ireland is Catholic and rainy, neither one very good for nude sunbathing.

6. Visiting a cathedral can be cathartic. (You don't have to actually believe the crap that caused it to be built.)

7. Church attendance might be fun in Haiti. Devil worship is optional.

8. Conde Nasty is <u>not</u> a guide to give your grand-mother.

9. Lesbian wives in Afghanistan are known to fancy men off to war.

10. Frequent flyers are also frequently unfaithful.

11. Filipino males tend to have dark Tootsie rolls, but suit yourself.

12. Russians are depressed, alcoholic, and in English can't keep their *the*'s, *a*'s, and *an*'s straight, yet they make lovely borscht.

13. Never ever tell an Australian to "zip it." (Just un-zip it.)

14. Make yourself at home in the USA. Overstaying your visa by a lifetime might be construed as rude.

15. A kiss on the hand may be quite Continental, but a bang in Bangkok ain't all bad.

16. Irish country life is picturesque and charming; still, it wears thin after forty years of self-abuse.

17. If you will suck off Her Majesty's horse guard, then you mustn't complain of an upset tummy.

By all means play your Gay Card whenever and wherever you may be – except in Uganda (and 83 other countries).

🐏 MORE WHAT NOT TO SAY ABOUT . . .

1. Tokyo . . . there's too much there there.

2. Oakland, California . . . it's Whitey's fault.

3. The San Francisco Gay Etc. Parade . . . is it truly, deeply boring, or is it just me?

4. The San Francisco Gay Etc. Parade . . . questioning, my ass!

5. The world can never have too many medical cures, nor too few religions.

6. Take all the gay rights in Muslim countries and stuff them up Osama Bin Ladin's dead ass, and you'll still have room left over most of Africa, most of the Middle East, and two Spike Lee films.

7. Robert Mugabe of Zimbabwe should be cooked and eaten by his countrymen, his homophobic heart cut out and stuffed in his mouth. (Stop making excuses for such people!)

8. You may comfort a forlorn sheep that is about to be shorn, but you cannot tell her that worse still awaits her.

9. Your general health is a subject we can all appreciate and relate to; nevertheless, the state of your bowels need not concern us at breakfast.

10. The Middle East . . . if you find it difficult, full of haggling and murder, just remember it's not you. It's *them*.

11. The Germans really are too much, but they make those Turks run on time.

12. There is undoubted homophobia among many Asians, but at least they don't write Rap songs about it.

13. When members of Ethnic Communities display severe homophobia, you must slap them on the wrist. (That is what they usually get.)

14. The Russians, Nigerians, Ugandans, and Palestinians don't think life it hard enough. They have to add anti-gay bigotry as icing.

WHAT IS TO BE SAID ABOUT CELEBS

1. O. J. Simpson . . . is he a lounge act at the Las Vegas Nugget yet?

2. Britney Spears . . . she who lives by the sword of pop sensibility dies by it.

3. Ian McKellen . . . shouldn't have worn that dress on "Saturday Night Live" or assault-kissed Jimmy Fallon. A great talent disgracing himself.

4. Pee Wee Herman (Paul Reuben) . . . got a raw deal. Let him who is without need for an orgasm cast the first stone.

5. Outed Star # 104 . . . we didn't get as far as we are because of cowards like you.

6. Elton John has had a memorial toilet named after him.

7. So has George Michael. (His career is in it.)

8. Sandra Bernhardt should do commercial for the Gap.

9. Michael Jackson. (Aside to poor, dead Michael Jackson: We all have had childhoods we didn't like. It doesn't mean we want to have slumber parties with nuns!)

10. The state of Brad Pitt's inner skeletal structure need not concern us overmuch.

11. We bet that if you hunt for "tabs" on Tab Hunter these days you'll find them.

12. Marlon Brando died because he ate a Pacific Island. (Or was it an islander?)

13. Siegfried and Roy . . . are real pussycats.

14. You have to hand it to Mel Gibson and his *Passion of the Christ*. He really knows how to make and market a 'snuff' film.

15. The modern singer Nelly doesn't appear to know what "nelly" means.

WHAT IS TO BE SAID AND HOW

1. Never say in any e-mail what you would not shout over a microphone in Times Square while playing the ukulele with your ass cheeks.

2. Elements of punctuation may not be entirely crucial for clarity, but they do show good breeding, however humble your origins.

3. Forwarding another's heartfelt sentiments that were sent to you alone to those in your Address Book does not show a noble mind.

4. It is now acceptable to use e-mail in order to 1) thank a friend for an enjoyable time together, 2) to fire an employee, 3) even to visit your elderly mother in that nursing home. But, really, you mustn't mass mail your obituary. There is enough SPAM already.

5. Irony, alas, is not possible without telegraphing it with graceless LOL's and Smiley Faces.

6. Say what you mean and mean what you say, because your e-mail lives somewhere in cyberspace for all eternity. Pace, Shakespeare the sonneteer!

7. "Cookies" are a necessary evil at times. Just don't spill yours on the keyboard.

8. FLAME NOT even if you are a Flamer.

9. One man's SPAM is another man's (a shut-in's) sex life.

🕊 THE ART OF VIDEO DATING

A. As the late Duchess of Windsor observed (or would have if video dating had been around when she was alive), in a video presentation one can never (appear to be) too rich or too diesel.

B. It is no longer necessary, we suppose, to ask permission of the fathers of the ones you are seeking to court before presenting your video.

C. It's not "procuring for an immoral purpose" if you send a video, except in certain Southern states or in countries with arranged marriages.

D. Mutual funds can cause a mutual attraction.

E. You may not use someone else 's video to attract a life partner. Eventually the other person will notice.

F. You may not use a video of someone else to reli eve yourself, only then to send it back and not even rewind.

G. You may send a video of a porn star and claim it is you. Do not be shocked if you are asked to display similar talents in person.

H. Video dating is no more unseemly, indeed is considerably less so, than having relatives pick sex partners (as in husbands and wives) for you to sleep with.

ODD SEXUAL KINKS AND HOW TO RESPOND

1. You thought you brought home Tex Ritter, or possibly Roy Rogers, but Sally Field somehow wound up in your bed. (Tell her you have admire her acting technique but have developed a headache.)

2. Filching doesn't mean I love you.

3. To rim or not to rim on the first date, particularly in Pacific Rim nations? *Hmm.*

4. One fellow's fetish is another culture's manners.

5. Dental dams are meant to prevent what exactly? Enjoyment?

6. Lesbians can have sex after Bed Death. As Nancy Reagan said, "Just do it!"

7. Paddling requires a regulation paddle. Violators are severely punished.

8. Riding sidesaddle is no longer required of even the most traditional of femmes.

9. Trannie grannies may find a stay in San Fran's Tenderloin a welcome change from Wichita Falls.

10. As the late Duchess of Windsor observed (or would have if sexual kinks had been around in her day) your sex slave can never be too rich or too thin.

11. Do lesbians go to Hooters?

12. Something tells us that Lesbian Piss Parties are a thing of the past.

13. But Piss Elegant Water Sports will never die.

14. Shit is never worn after Labor Day.

15. If you ask someone what he'd like to do, and he says fuck your ass and then watch you suck his shitty dick off, followed by pissing in your mouth, the proper response is "Not just now, thanks."

16. Listening to anti-gay reggae music whole doing your houseboy of color is so Twentieth Century!

🦋 SHOULD ONE GOSSIP??

1. Gossip is always terribly wrong. (But do it anyway!)

2. Did you hear? Melissa Ethridge, k.d. laing, and Dolly Parton are forming a new trio, to be called the Lesbian Country Supremes, their first release *Gal Tunes*.

3. The Pope is gay, or maybe it's just his gowns.

4. Tom Cruise is not gay. Tom Cruise is not gay. Tom Cruise is not gay.

5. Bruce Villanch is not gay.

6. Whoopi Goldberg is not Jewish.

7. Whoopi Goldberg invented the Goldberg Cushion.

8. 8. Julian Clary, the British comic, got in trouble for saying that he fisted a fat Parliamentarian (Norman LeMond, now a lord). He should have held his piece instead.

9. Roy Cohn was not gay. He was pre-gay.

10. John Travolta is not gay. He just sometimes has sex with men.

11. Kevin Spacey is not spacey.

COSMETIC SURGERY

1. A poor image can make you want to conquer Europe and can be helped by lifts in your shoes, full DaVinci caps, and a butt tuck.

2. You may have the fat removed, via liposuction, from your love handles, lower abdomen, and chin – never from your penis, unless it is a transfusion for a friend.

3. DaVinci caps on your teeth don't necessarily make you a genius.

4. Your unsightly gums are your business, naturally, until such time as you choose to expose them in that frightening smile.

5. Breast enhancements will not remedy your shrill feminist tone.

6. A new nose need not necessitate nosiness.

7. Rhinoplasty will not help if you truly resemble a rhinoceros.

8. "Titties on men" is not a line from "My Favorite Things."

9. Stretch marks could conceivably mean, "Steve, you shouldn't have had his baby."

10. Photo-facials remove age spots, but they sting like neocon Wasps. We tell you this because the beauty brochures won't.

11. Lady Hammer once had a ThermaLift on her face. "It was one hour of intense agony, but I did look three or four days younger!" she reported. Her Ladyship is ever the optimist, but try not to have cosmetic treatments that last longer than the results!

COSMETIC SURGERY – AGAIN

~ *one can never have too much!*

1. Gravity will not be defied forever. Do what you may, each buttock will droop, just not at the same time.

2. A tummy tuck may help in your belly dancing aspirations, yet one can only accomplish so much without dancing lessons.

3. Your bulbous butt cheeks? Like marriage, what God has joined together let no man put asunder? (We feel it is silly advice about both marriage and bulbous butt cheeks.)

4. Body sculpting probably will not make you into a Michelangelo model.

5. Cheek implants can make you cheeky, if you don't watch yourself.

6. Liposuction cannot hide a peasant fondness for Taco Bell.

7. Broad backs, not broad minds, are proletarian in the extreme!

8. Chin implants, cheek implants, and breast implants as well? Are you sure you wouldn't

rather try reincarnation? (There's usually an office two doors down.)

9. Botox removes wrinkles in the brow, but is it doesn't last forever, the way Love does.

10. Graves are fine and private places. But none, I think, do there wear braces. (So take them off before you die.)

11. Remember, Botox up the buttocks will give you a wrinkle-free asshole. (For what it's worth. . . . Only you can decide.)

12. A comb-over is no substitute for hair implants, or sincerity.

13. Your hair plugs should never be used in conjunction with your butt plugs. You could implode.

AT THE GYM

1. Where is it?

2. Do we have to go?

3. You go!

4. Paunches are not that bad.

5. One doesn't want that false, pumped-up look! All should be natural, as Rousseau so wisely noted.

6. Think positive! It's only 245 sit-ups for each profiterole!

7. Work on lowering that voice, or all those pommel gyrations are for naught.

8. A scream from the pain of 35 bench presses, yes, but from seeing a mouse, never!

9. Triceps, biceps! Really now, don't neglect to exercise the penis as strenuously as your other bodily parts.

10. Sweat is apparently an accompaniment of vigorous physical exercise, but it need not be collected in a jar and left in a locker as a testament to your achievements.

11. You cannot use the rowing machine and the candy machine at the same time.

12. Be gentle with the equipment. It is not its fault that you still haven't found a lover.

OUR HANDICAPPED BRETHREN

(AND SISTREN)

1. In that dark back room all cats are black. If you remain very still, no one need judge you because of your wheelchair.

2. Buy a Lark maybe, even a Rascal. But what's with the Daytona 500 race car?

3. A Groping Room for the gay blind isn't as politically incorrect as it may sound.

4. White canes are not (I repeat not) used after Labor Day.

5. Crutches can be overlooked, if festooned with rainbow flags.

6. You may not have a bumper sticker proclaiming: Jesus Is My Crutch.

7. Freddy Kruger is hot! (Tell yourself that.)

8. Wheelchair access can lead to wheelchair excess. Curb your cruising!

9. Do not run down that meter maid for ticketing you while cruising the park, however much you are tempted and the bitch deserves it.

10. You may not abuse your "otherwise-abled" footman, though slow to move your luggage, because times have changed. You don't have to tip him, however. (Don't trip him either.)

11. You may not slap a saucy maid, unless you are insured, or Lady Hammer.

12. You may read the menu to the mentally disabled, but they should be permitted to feed themselves.

13. Listen closely to the raving maniac in the adjoining toilet stall. He may be trying to tell you something.

14. Do not stare at the handicapped – unless they are blind and can't see you.

15. You may not cruise when you have Alzheimer's, unless on a leash.

THE BEAR ESSENTIALS

A. You are not fat and ugly. You're a bear!

B. Facial hair can repair what Mother Nature failed to place in that chin.

C. You can't be both a linebacker and Prom Queen, except on Gay Day or alternate Fridays.

D. "Mary" was a little bear.
Its fleece was dark as dye.
And everywhere that "Mary" went
Her bear was sure to lie.

E. Bear women? Complete baldness in women tends to be an affectation.

F. Heavyset is de *rigueur* in this milieu, but Sumo Wrestler Bears? We think not! It's mixing the genres.

G. You can be butch without carrying a chainsaw to the pub.

H. He who wears lace panties under his overalls is not playing the game fairly.

I. Most gay men are masculine, contrary to the world's woeful ignorance. The nelly simply are more noticeable. Nelly bears are the most noticeable of all.

MORE TRAVEL TIPS

1. On airplanes, the young children of gays and lesbians have no more right to be obnoxious than those of their heterosexual counterparts. Nor less.

2. When traveling in Islamist countries, always be sure to tick at least one of your preferred death penalty options for being gay: a) flogged to death or b) thrown from a cliff — so as to have the choice you truly, truly want and not have it made for you.

3. Jokes about the Holocaust are in bad taste, except in Arab countries.

4. Motel 6, no doubt, has lovely letterhead stationery; still, one must not use it for one's résumé.

5. You can too be happy staying at a castle all by yourself, with only your own good company and the entire staff to cheer you!

6. England has bugs, yes, but they are much better behaved than most other bugs.

7. Bees can make it on their own without help from your un-looked-after armpits.

8. God bless Merrie Old England! It still has signs like The Fund for Brain-Injured Infants.

9. When asked to remove portions of your clothing at an airport checkpoint, it is not necessary to wiggle or dance as you go through the metal detector.

10. It is also not proper to wave the removed clothing over your head, however festive your holiday.

11. If you are stranded on a desert island, your best hope for a companion is a boat builder who likes to give blowjobs.

12. Gordon Square in London without its greenery would be as charmless as Virginia Woolf without "her" bush.

13. Moscow in winter is as alluring as a van full of dead pigs.

14. A catamaran to Capri is usually preferable to a donkey to Detroit.

15. Sorry. Gypsies are not good role models.

DINING OUT

1. One so tires of being wealthy and dining in the finest restaurants, doesn't one?

2. "Hello, I'm Eric, and I'll be your server tonight" is not always a pick- up line.

3. "Check, please!" does not imply that you are demanding an assignation with the waiter from Prague. (Unless it does!)

4. One can dine "out" without announcing that one is gay to all around you!

5. As the late Duchess of Windsor observed, one's belches, like one's steaks, can never be too rare.

6. One burp during dinner is forgivable if masked by your napkin and a brief apology. Two or more burps mean ostracism to Sizzler.

7. Contrary to folklore, King Arthur and Guinevere did not serve pizza at the original Round Table.

8. A bodily function like passing wind is completely natural, as our good friend Lady Hammer likes to point out, but one need not fly a kite at supper.

9. As for silverware, begin with the utensils on the outside and work inward, and don't take them

to your room for cooking your heroin. Let the servants bring them to you.

10. You should no more smoke in a dining room than fart in a saint's tomb.

11. You may dine in the stables only if the stable boy is serving it up.

12. After four courses, one does rather look piggish if one pinches extra chocolates with the coffee in the lounge.

13. A roulade is not a Rolaid. Quite the contrary. And demanding either of your host is unmannerly.

14. Small animal grunts of satisfaction with your food are acceptable if you are Princess Margaret of England, and only if.

15. If the music is "The Girl from Emphysema" you know it's a smoking-permitted establishment.

16. When Brazil 66 sings "The Girl from Ipanema" for the third time on the Muzak it's time to go.

POLITE PENILE ENHANCEMENT

1. Do you really think there's a pill that can add three inches to your member? Get over it, Alice! Drug counseling available!

2. "Cut" vs. "uncut" continues to be a debate in editing rooms across the world and will perhaps never be resolved.

3. A piece of head-cheese-laden flesh may be a delicacy for a certain type of connoisseur, but some have made this into a religion, and we already have more than enough religions.

4. Circumcision is no worse than that head cheese catcher you're so proud of!

5. We met a man who said he'd had penile enlargement, but you could have fooled us.

6. Can one have a penis reduction, as with breasts, for those of us for whom it is a concern? . . . (*Shut up!*)

7. *Cialis* rhymes with *phallus*, but it doesn't hold a candle to *Vitalis* (at least when you're thirteen and just pubescing).

8. Yes, you can overdose on Viagra. It is the method preferred by the Hemlock Society.

9. The foreskin of the Baby Jesus has preoccupied Medieval scholars (and no one else with any sense) for millennia.

10. The best enhancement of the male member is an agreeable and thorough lover, of one's month's duration.

11. Length is not everything. There is also girth – and presentation.

12. Never suck a penis that has been artificially enlarged, anymore than you would eat chemically engineered cucumbers. (But one can only tell from a taste test.)

13. A strap, strategically placed in the nether regions, can keep a flagging tryst alive, just like a smile at a sorority tea party.

BRUSH UP YOUR LATIN

1. *O tempora! O mores!* (Translation: Nobody studies Latin anymore!)

2. There is truth in *vitro* as well as in *vino*.

3. *De gustibus non est disputandem*: example: having a sex change from male to female in order to become a lesbian.

4. *Ad hoc* is not a German beer. It's a Belgian ale used to seduce passing schoolboys, over the age of consent, of course, depending on the country.

5. *Quid pro quo* is not British money paid to a rent boy. (Unless it is!)

6. *Sic transit gloria mundi* is not Latin for the perfect subway glory hole, especially busy on Mondays.

7. *RIP*: for some the only Latin they ever learn is on their tombstone.

8. *Habemus Papam* means "We have a new Pope" (to fuck gay people over some more)

9. *Non compos mentis* means drag queens on Ecstasy.

10. *Annus mirabilis.* Well, smell you!

11. *Annus horribilis.* Spare us the details of your tragic sphincter.

12. *Homo sum*: I am a homo.

13. *Tempus fugit*. (Translation: Time fucks you over.)

CRUISES

1. *Bon voyage! Bon chance! Bon mots!* . . . You're still Burvel Stuckey from Enid, Oklahoma.

2. As my good friend Lady Hammer always says, "Staff rather enjoy changing your reservations six or seven times, and, further, it keeps them off the streets!"

3. The flag reads Norwegian, so why is the crew to a man Malaysian? (The Better Business Bureau is absolutely no help here.)

4. "I'll skip the basket of bread and have the chef's basket instead!" is not in Amy Vanderbilt.

5. Excessive tipping is expected, as are sea sickness and multiple vomitings.

6. A quickie in the "head" is not a shipboard romance.

7. You would no more dine with the crew than you would, one hopes, engage in hanky panky with them.

8. If you drop a morsel on your shirt at the Captain's Table, you may redeem yourself if you faint from embarrassment.

9. "Is there anything to be done about this vanilla?!" is a comment that may serve you well if expressed in your native German. In English it sounds more Hitlerian than upper class.

10. In the lifeboat, it's boy, girl, boy, girl, except for the occasional empty spaces for those eaten by sharks.

WINE AND DINE YET AGAIN

1. At a formal dinner one never likes to hear certain words. These include the conventional curse words as well as "our customers' needs." The airing of the imperatives of "commerce" can quite take the chill off the nicest sorbet.

2. Stroking the hand of the fetching lad who is serving your crème brule may not be as obvious an overture as you think. Suck his cock or nothing – but not until after coffee in the lounge.

3. Whilst in the United Kingdom, in two weeks or less, after the large breakfasts, the large luncheons, the afternoon teas, and the evening suppers, you could very well begin to look like Henry VIII.

4. Inclement weather need not deter the practicing lesbian from eating out al *fresco*.

5. If one farts among company, the appropriate response is to ignore it and say nothing, as should others, unless you have blown out the candles.

6. One fart at a formal dinner is a misfortune. Two in a row are *gauche* beyond measure. More than three and you may claim that you have invented a new parlor game for all to participate in.

7. Fine wine is like fine conversation, best left to the experts.

8. You may no longer take advantage of the hall boy as you pass along the corridors of a manor house, unless you are peckish.

9. Plaque on one's teeth from a lifetime of inattention probably cannot be removed by vigorous personal oral stimulation. (But try the oral stimulation anyway.)

10. If you are invited to Downton Abbey for lunch, for Heaven's sake don't go. (It's a TV show, my dear.)

OF POLITICS

1. Politics, whether plural or singular – and one can never remember! – is or are a dreary business, and that is all that's to be said of politics!

2. A liberal is one who can't ever see the bad in people, while a conservative is one who can't ever trust the good.

3. Liberals, you cannot embrace *both* gay rights and Islamic fundamentalists!

4. Liberals can't seem to understand that they will be the first to go if religious extremists have their way.

5. Conservatives say they believe in limited government, but apparently they make exceptions for, sex, drugs, and a whole Constitutional amendment to ban gay marriage.

6. Conservatives conserve, especially their money.

7. Churches who cause and uphold discrimination and hatred against gays should have their pets and their tax exempt status neutered.

8. The Phelps Family of Kansas, who says God loves them and puts 'God Hates Gays' on their protest signs, is right. So close that Old Testament and

have a thought or two of your own on the subject.

9. Orthodox Jews are for separation of Church and State. (Right up there with their Gay Rights Plank)

10. Conservative Dykes for Bush . . . is probably not a political statement.

🕊️ TRANSLATIONS

1. "I want to be your snowbird" ("I can't get a Green Card on my own.")

2. "I want you to be my meal ticket" (must be a hidden message.)

3. "Death to infidels" translates from Arabic as "We are moderates!"

4. "Americans Go Home!" (But leave your laptops.)

5. "We despise the evil United States of America." (Why are the lines so long to get in then?)

6. "I fancy your body." ("But why is your fanny pack so hard to remove?!")

7. "I stole your place in line. Ha, ha!" (Your response: "In America we shoot people for less. Ha, ha!"

8. "You Americans are so stupid! We are better than you any day!" (And it's the Americans who are supposed to be ugly?)

9. "Kiss me. I am desirous of you." ("Only fifty Euros for the first minute, twenty Euros per minute after that.")

10. "Oh, sir, you dropped this money at the ATM." ("Take it while my thieving partner swipes your debit card from the ATM slot.")

11. Amnesty? I know, I know, you're only here because you want to vote against gay marriage.

⟡ INNIGRATIONS

1. I'll clean yours if you'll clean mine.

2. Yes, you learned to circumvent bureaucracy in the Soviet Bloc, but here you are supposed to *earn* that bachelor's degree.

3. What is so rare as a Russian smile?

4. If I wanted to speak Spanish I'd go to Spain.

5. If I wanted a Tower of Babel I'd go there.

6. If Americans can speak English badly, so can you.

7. Welcome from Asia! We don't have enough smokers here already!

8. Native customs, such as spitting on the street, are charming only on your native soil, if then.

9. Most people are too polite to tell you your eleven children are not God's plan, just your loose loins.

10. We can see how you rhapsodize about what a great country America is since you grandparents on both sides as well as four uncles and two nephews are living on Social Security they never paid into.

11. I know, I know, you're only here because you want to commit crimes that Americans don't want to commit.

12. We won't help to deport you if you cease your raging homophobia.

13. Funny, you let very few immigrants into *your* countries.

OUTING THE DEAD

1. It is obvious now that Joan of Arc was a butch number, with more than a touch of schizophrenia to lead her on her way. Too bad she fought for France and not Gay Rights.

2. Johnnie Ray was the nelly "priest" in *There's No Business Like Show Business*, but Dan Dailey, the father in the same movie, it is now known, should have been known as Dan Dally.

3. Danny Kaye. Johnnie Ray, and Sir Laurence Olivier all had names that rhyme with A! (which was part of the Secret Code that Rhymes with gay) Hurray!

4. Attila the Hun was once somebody's bottom, and, yes, he was called "hon."

5. The Pied Piper of Hamlin was a chicken hawk.

6. Romeo liked young girls.

7. Marilyn Monroe took orders from Paula Strasberg.

8. Cary Grant and Randolph Scott shared a house in Hollywood, but they had separate beds, since Randolph liked to wear his spurs to bed and Cary did not.

9. Frederick the Great was merely adequate in bed.

10. Liberace wasn't gay. He just sounded that way because he was devoted to his mother.

11. The director of Frankenstein, James Whale, had a thing for big boys with big bolts in their necks.

12. What was Victoria's secret? She was a trannie! *Quelle surprise!*

13. All male organists, living or dead, at some time have played the organ.

14. Leonardo DaVinci never married, had a young boy companion, and added another male companion as the years wore on. But of course he was not gay!

 # THE FINEST NAMES

~ *should you change yours?*

Lady Blindsummit is obviously of the most aristocratic of origins.

Lord Corrosive may be a crank, but his family does date back to Norman the Conqueror. (*Who?*)

Lady Flitwick could only be of the highest breed of drag queen.

The Marquis of Fisting Upon Heathrow is not your average bloke.

Lord Whineforth is of that unfortunate class, the penniless with a title.

Princess Snootful was the servants' name for the late Princess Margaret of Great Britain.

You must never forget your place with the earl of Great Looting. After all, quite naturally he is proud of his family's origins.

If saying the name of the town Cockermouth aloud excites you, you must be about eight years old.

High Hiccough is not a good address.

Leeking Arsehope is an even worse address and best avoided by the nearest roundabout.

Stroking-on-Thyme is quite close to Wanking on the Green.

Sir Neville Cockforth started out as a mere yeoman, but he somehow made his way up in society.

Family backgrounds are often revealed by surnames, as in Baker, Cook, and Clark. One might consider legally changing one's name if it is any of those or even unfortunate ones like Dickson, Peterson, or Foote.

LAWSUITS

1. Litigious leprechauns have little dicks.

2. Lawsuits are to be avoided unless you are new-fangled feminist upset because your property has been entailed to a distant male cousin. (Otherwise a duel is still the preferred method of settling a dispute.)

3. Lesbian duels are usually the most colorful and the most accurate.

4. The Law and homosexuals rarely see eye to eye, and yet that should not stop you from having a jolly good time, if you are discreet and also know how to bribe police officials.

5. A lawyer, like that "trick" in the cloak room, is not your friend until you pay him.

6. Ever since the trials of Oscar Wilde, it has been advisable not to sue people who can't spell "sodomite."

7. When and if Congress fully includes gays as a protected class under the Hate Crimes Statues, we will be sure not to abuse our former abusers, being the ladies and gentlemen that we are.

8. Women are beaten to death for flirting with a man who is not their husband in certain parts of

the world, and in America a woman can sue a man without cause and suffer no penalty at all to herself.

9. Your "privates" may at times require a *Public* Defender.

10. Yes, you should sue that plainclothes Vice Squad officer for going and spoiling your gay cruise.

11. Stable boys are not as stable as you may like, nor should they be actual "boys" if you are seeking gratification rather than litigation.

CULTIVATING THOSE MUSICAL ARTS

1. One can still be a gay man and not like opera one little bit!

2. Like kangaroo, Australian opera is an acquired taste.

3. Counter-tenors are sissies. (But don't get into a screaming match with one.)

4. Yet counter-tenors, it is rumored, often demand to be "Tops."

5. Twelve-tone operas are, like unsafe sex, most enjoyed from a great distance.

6. Aural pleasure is one of the few remaining comforts of the over-ninety set. (So stick it in their ear.)

7. Be sure it is the maestro's baton protruding from the orchestra pit before pointing it out to your Great Aunt Augusta.

8. You rarely find louts at the opera, although at times those noisy curtain calls do go on and on!

9. *The Magic Flute* is gay code for oral sex in the top row of the Metropolitan Opera House.

10. Beverly Sills is not to be confused with Beverly Hills, though approximately the same size.

11. If your guests are finding it hard to sleep, play them several Prokofiev art songs based on Pushkin.

12. Contraltos should be seen and not heard. (Most of them shouldn't be seen either.)

13. On radio stations of the future, Rap will be divided into three types: Classical, Easy-Listening, and Light, with Smooth Rap a distinct fourth possibility. So those who fear for the future of music need have no worries.

14. Did we really need this – *Snoop Dogg – the Opera*?

15. Rap is more of a cultural/political art form than pure music, as well as a method of employment for the underclass who cannot sing.

16. Castrati make the best Rap singers, although they are harder and harder to find; nevertheless, it is a custom to consider reviving.

THOSE SENIOR MOMENTS

1. If you inadvertently double dose on your Viagra, call 911 and tell them to send two hunky, strong paramedics equipped with the Jaws of Life.

2. You are never too old for an orgasm. You just may not notice when it occurs. Stay awake and take notes.

3. You are having a senior moment if you believe you are receiving head from Pretty Boy Floyd.

4. Senile dementia is not as bad as it sounds. You forget why you went down when that Young Thing walks away.

5. The end of life is matched by the beginning of life: gumless suckings, both best cherished as memories than photographed by relatives.

6. "Depends" need not be drab. Fashion is the task master always for both the outside and inside of one's clothing.

7. Prostate enlargement is a turn-on for few.

8. Frequent urination is not a problem if you frequent Tea Rooms.

9. One may fall asleep at the opera but not in mid-toy boy.

10. As with the department of Motor Vehicles and vision, one must have one's eyes checked in order to cruise safely. One clearly does not want to suck off a fire hydrant or a Dudley Moore impersonator.

11. Though costly, having one's butt cheeks aligned every forty thousand rotations is not a bad idea.

12. Pre-mature ejaculation is not only the sincerest form of flattery; it gives the impression that you are sixteen, to say nothing of getting you to sleep by nine-thirty.

13. The elderly should always have sexual relations on the first date. There may be no more!

14. Sexual activity will likely decrease with age; still, if it has been more than seventy years you are probably dead.

15. Seniors, remember: the Levitra first, the cockstrap second, and the orgasm third.

16. Years from now, when Lady Gaga really is ga-ga, be kind.

17. We had several hundred more sparkling bits of advice. (But they seem to have slipped our mind.)

☙ OUR TRANNIE FRIENDS

A.   A. Merely cutting off one's penis in a snit does not qualify you for transgender legal status. One must also cultivate a certain feminine mystique.

B.   Most transvestites tend to be cross-dressing heterosexuals – yes, I've got that. And transsexuals identify as the opposite sex and alter their bodies to suit their souls – I've got that one too. However, what on earth are Questioning Trannies? (It would drive Miss Manners to distraction too.)

C.   The term is trans-person, or a person of trans-ness – nothing else, no matter what you may have heard on the street.

D.   Do any gay people actually have sex with trans-persons? Isn't it a heterosexual fetish?

E.   Always tell your sexual partners that you used to be the other sex, particularly if you want to be beaten to death with a frying pan.

F. Of course you're PROUD. You're a lipstick-wearing, plus-sized homely man in a dress with one leg shorter than the other. Why wouldn't you be?! But are placards at the State Fair truly necessary?

THE UPPER CLASSES

~ can you handle them?

1. Princess Diana was too tall for Prince Charles and shouldn't have married beneath her.

2. Princess Diana is buried at Althorpe on a small island surrounded by a series of small gnomes resembling Elton John.

3. Princess Di was killed because she was carrying Elton John's child.

4. A lady's name appears in the newspapers only three times in her lifetime: when she is born, when she marries . . . and when she turns lesbian.

5. You can recognize genuine "class" when you have been thoroughly fucked and yet you don't feel a thing except a nice glow.

6. You are "common" when you don't even know what "common" means.

7. You make yourself "common" when you fist the gardener.

8. Snuff is no longer snorted in the best houses after formal dinner parties.

9. The Duke of High Sandwich's stories may make him seem like an old bore, no matter how long his pedigree. Still, his willie may be a different story.

10. Old money doesn't smell. New money does.

11. The Duchess of Levittown is probably *nouveau riche.*

12. The late Princess Margaret pre-deceased her mother, the "Queen Mum," by several years, and her own reputation by decades.

13. The upper classes may cease to be delightful if you guillotine them.

14. One grows so dreadfully weary of having others wait on one hand and foot. (But if one waits, this feeling passes.)

15. Even a "two-gun maharajah" should never be addressed with "Howdy!"

16. Camilla Parker Bowles never eats the crust of her brie. Nor should you if you expect to nab a prince.

17. It was bad enough when they made that shopkeeper's daughter Lady Thatcher!

18. But it's all over when it's Dame Britney Spears.

LIVING WITH OXYMORONS
(AND OTHER MORONS)

1. Public education in America.

2. East German décor.

3. Lesbian fashions.

4. Remember, gays do not have to lower their standards whilst bringing about the Fall of Western Civilization.

5. How can so many darling British babies turn into so many homely adults?

6. Can one may raise one's standards while lowering a tradesman's livery?

7. American children are often embarrassed by their parents, but apparently never by their clothing.

8. Sad to see: a dumb gay man. Alas, they do exist.

9. Bare-backing, like a boy band, does not improve with age.

10. Surprise, surprise! Some gay men are handy even with tools that are not their own!

11. We have been informed by our editor that the rest of this list would upset the Masses and the Middle Class, so it has been abridged.

THE WINE SNOB

1. "Dyke Wine Bar" summons up jarring images.

2. Do not tip the wine steward, unless he is already tipping.

3. House wines tend not to be one hundred years old, except in the Mini Bar at Motel 6.

4. A light blush (or a rosé) is suitable for your already-drunk granny.

5. Do not say, "Gimme one them 'C' wines," when you wish a Chablis, a Chardonnay, or a Claret.

6. Even a superficial knowledge of delirium tremors is better than no knowledge at all.

7. Ireland is lovely, but Irish wine is not.

8. Old, world-weary people make the best wine experts, and the best winos.

9. How can one tell a wine snob from a wino? The wine snot spits *after* he drinks, and the wino *before*.

10. You may spit wine out only if you are a wine judge in an international competition, or in the parking lot of Sizzler.

11. You may not gargle a Chateau Lafitte; you may a Listerine 2006.

12. It never hurts to smile when you vomit on yourself.

13. Twist caps are gauche, even in the homes of Hip Hop stars.

14. In *vino* not only is there *veritas*, there is also possible Traffic School.

15. Wine stains *do* come out, if you have an experienced tongue.

16. You let red wines "breathe" because . . . somebody said so a long time ago.

17. Whites are chilled, but never made into Popsicles.

18. *Vin ordinaire* does not mean a bottle of Ripple in your U-Haul!

19. Leftover wine bottles are best disposed of, rather than left around the palace as mementos.

WHAT TO SAY TO YOUR BEHIND-THE-TIMES RELATIVES

1. About your gayness, when they say, "Well, it's a choice you made," say, "Yes, at the same time you chose to be an asshole."

2. When your sister and her husband say, "Which one of you two is the male in your relationship, you reply, "Which is the male in yours?"

3. When your cousin the Catholic priest says, "But you're so promiscuous!" you say, "Never? You mean you really never have sex of any kind? Not even rubbing against the sheets?!" (or the odd altar boy?)

4. When your Orthodox rabbi brother-in-law quotes Leviticus to you, pull his curls.

5. When they refer to having "Zero Tolerance for those sort of people," say, "How many times must you be told not to mention your I.Q. score!"

6. When your uncle the Imam quotes a fatwa at you, tell him you are on a low *fat-wa* diet.

7. If you are invited to give the commencement speech at an Islamist *madras* boys' school, bring

your Barbra Streisand albums with you, whether or not you play them as background music.

8. Your Irish Catholic relatives want you to make a pilgrimage to Lourdes to rid yourself of your homosexuality. Tell them you'll go if it still has a Club Baths.

9. No, *Brokeback Mountain* didn't win Best Picture. So Armageddon is not quite here yet.

MORE WINE

1. Toasts: "To Her Majesty's health!" is always proper, unless Her Majesty has just died face down in her shepherd's pie.

2. "Up yours!" is often mistaken in the finest homes even when it is merely said to encourage stock investments.

3. After-dinner liqueurs are consumed only by alcoholic toddlers, as is liquor in candy!

4. One may indulge in the occasional aperitif before fisting.

5. "Wine, women, and song" are the perfect trio for your gay male orgy, even if you omit just one element.

6. Sir, lesbian three-ways are best enjoyed with an inexpensive wine by yourself in the Super 8 Motel in Jackson Hole, Wyoming or in the pages of *Playboy* magazine.

7. Shirazes, like Spike Lee films, are over-rated.

8. Sniff the cork, if you must, but not the *sommelier*.

9. Merlot is not the name of the wizard in tales of the Round Table.

10. 10. If your "Life is a Cabernet!" you may be in serious trouble.

🦑 ON AIRPLANES

1. Peanuts are no longer handed out to all, lest a peanut-phobic passenger have a reaction. By the same principle, no bad meals henceforth will ever be served to any plane's manifest. (Yeah, sure.)

2. The pilot may not drink while flying; still, he is permitted copious quantities of the co-pilot's cum, if both are hot and we can watch.

3. You may not speak to the person in the seat next to you; however, you may fiddle with their seatbelt if asked.

4. When the steward insists that you fasten your seatbelt tightly and then helps you, he is not signaling a post-flight dalliance in the realms of Sado-Masochism. (It could mean a mid-flight dalliance!)

5. Do not try to masturbate in the lavatory or you may trigger the anti-smoking device, and all Hell will descend upon you.

6. Copulating on a plane is really only for those rare occasions when it is a troop carrier and you are welcoming the boys back home.

7. You may be bumped up to First Class if you bump the purser, especially if you are cute and he is not.

8. Adult movies are not yet available on flights; however, you may politely ask the nearest male flight attendant to dance naked for you in the aisle.

9. Conversations, like you with your seatbelt, should be restrained in flight.

10. Long trips are inconvenient but necessary, as Magellan and Christopher Columbus well knew.

11. It's not just all sex, sex, sex with gay men! We also enjoy peanuts – if we could get some!

APHORISMS TO LIVE BY

1. Having known toothache, one can understand religion.

2. Having had a child in youth, one can expect loneliness in old age.

3. The closer one gets to London, the less the service.

4. A civilization that opens its borders too widely, because its citizens want to have their houses cleaned and their sex drive sated, is on its way to extinction. – the New Cicero.

5. Where are those border patrols when the pickets' signs say *Illegal Immigrants Against Gay Marriage*?!

6. Wisdom, like wealth, is what we want our children to have, since we didn't have it ourselves.

7. You will regret not having children. (Or having them.)

8. You will always regret not having had a lover. (Or having one as well.)

9. If you tend to ejaculate too readily, delay pleasure. Have sex with corpses.

10. Home-schooled probably does not mean a gay-friendly curriculum.

11. Five of your babies in hand and one in the oven says you've delighted yourself quite enough.

12.

A disdainful stare
can keep
many a dog
in his place.

LOUTS

1. They hardly deserve a whole page of this guide, but their numbers seem to be growing, and so we must acknowledge their existence.

2. In certain locales, don't be fooled by their hairnets. They are still louts.

3. Never underestimate the inexpressible rage of drunken, macho males who think you are getting more sex than they are.

4. It is no longer possible to discourage loutish behavior with a stern look or a gentle cough of warning. Nowadays one must rely on other measures. But even a stun gun can be employed with finesse. (But do not bother with the niceties.)

5. Yes, you are a lout, and you must apologize by taking it doggy style!

6. Louts can be avoided by staying away from certain sporting events, or from most family gatherings.

7. Do not become loutish yourself when dispensing justice to the unruly. Kill them quietly.

8. You may recognize a lout even before encountering pronounced lout-like behavior. He will be reading the *abridged* Ronald Firbank.

9. You may recognize a group of louts (a litter of louts) in advance, and thus prevent untoward incidents, for they will be either a) picking their noses, b) grabbing their crotches, or c) not wearing Armani.

10. It is not an absolute sign of loutishness to wear your trousers at mid-buttock or below, but you will find it difficult to deliver your State of the Union address so attired.

🐏 MORE AIRPLANES

1. You may sit by an EXIT only if you are strong enough to open the door in an emergency, or if you wish to show off those muscles so diligently worked on at the gym.

2. You may have one carry-on piece of luggage – and one carry-off co-pilot.

3. You cannot get frequent flyer credit for your Mile High Membership.

4. While watching the in-flight movie, no matter how aroused you may get, you may not move from seat to seat as you would in your favorite porn haunt.

5. Lavatories on airplanes rarely have glory holes, and thus should be complained of vigorously to the management.

6. To lessen the tedium of a long air journey, fondle your nipples at every stop-over, preferably privately or in a like-minded group.

7. If your plane crashes, you may be entitled to a refund, if you fill out the form in triplicate. (But only before you leave.)

8. If terrorists hijack your plane, promptly remove your Gay Liberation Now button.

9. If your seat-mate will not cease his or her ceaseless chatter, slap them silly.

10. Airline staff take "jokes" about bombs very seriously. So before you board stuff your wit where the sun don't shine.

☙ DORM LIFE

1. Upon arrival at hall you will receive an inventory of your room. Before departure, examine it for towels, bed sheets, pillow cases, and crabs, for you will be held responsible for all and sundry.

2. You will be supplied with a single bed, two sheets, two pillow cases, and a duvet with cover at the beginning of term. If you do not know what a duvet is, your manservant will, and hence he can attend to it.

3. Religious enthusiasts of any type are not permitted to wander the halls seeking converts; however, they may receive a tax break from the U.S. Government.

4. Ground floor windows are often secured by catches to preserve them from opening more than six inches. If you experience erections of greater proportions, you must leave or enter by a higher window.

5. One must not flaunt one's erections, however inspiring, unless one is at home with a partner, or at a certified YMCA.

6. Drug dealers and addicts, many of whom are disturbed, may rendezvous erratically outside

your dormitory, and thus you must be first in line for quick service.

7. Only one guest is allowed to remain in hall after 11:00 P.M., up from no guests from just a few years ago. So one must pay the overnight Orgy Registration Fee at the reception desk *before* 11: 00 P.M.!

8. If you bring back a handsome "trick," who, upon examination in the reception area, appears to be crazed beyond repair, ask the reception clerk to tell your would-be guest that you have disappeared because you "are just resting."

9. Please consider others when you are playing your stereo or engaging in Sado-Masochistic practices. Stereos should be turned down and instructions to your sex slave kept to a whisper.

10. Corridors are communal areas, but they are not for social gatherings. Confine your cruising to suitable places, such as the Internet or a nearby mosque.

11. If you do not let the staff know, how can they put it right? Therefore, always inform them of malfunctioning elevators and broken condoms.

12. It is not the reception clerk's responsibility to cut your Viagra pills into two pieces. Bring your own paraphernalia. Or bite the bullet.

13. If you overdose on Levitra at a Youth hostel, you have no one to blame but yourself. You ignored that discount at Elder Hostel!

14. Residents are required to pack up and remove all their belongings at the end of each term, including the summer term. If you have nowhere to go because you have no friends and will not speak to your relatives, you can still redeem yourself by writing a gay etiquette manual.

🐾 ILLEGAL AND DANGEROUS ACTIVITIES

A. Use of drugs during Gay Day at Disneyland just makes the Right Wing righter.

B. Vandalizing Lorna Luft at her concert honoring her mother, Judy Garland, will result in immediate expulsion.

C. Killing the Lesbian Vice Squad officer who has arrested you for cruising is ungentlemanly. Wait a couple of years and she will probably be up on domestic violence charges herself.

D. There is no need for further advice in these areas, as gays and lesbians, bisexuals, transgenders, and questioning always, always obey the law.

E. One, however, cannot be so sure about those Questionings!

PROPER DRAG

1. The courtyard of a good motel is always a good choice for crowning the Empress of Dayton.

2. Drag competitions are best held indoors, in places like Budget Inn in Shreveport, never in soccer stadiums, except possibly in Amsterdam.

3. A man in drag is always hilarious; a woman out of women's clothes is always dangerous.

4. Drag queens in Kabul are required to wear the complete burqa. No slacking off.

5. Even the Christian group known as The Promise Keepers must book early for its half-time drag entertainment.

6. "Girlie man" though she may be, in your heart of hearts you know that you don't want to get into a fistfight with a drag queen.

🖤 POLICE

A. Gays and lesbians now serve on some metropolitan police forces. They are still "pigs" and should be addressed as such. (But only when they are safely stun-gunned or otherwise secured.)

B. There is no lower form of gay life than a bull dyke cop who arrests gay men for cruising.

C. There are lies, damned lies, and Vice Squad reports.

D. Offer to accompany any Vice Squad officers who are also arresting heterosexuals humping in their cars. (Fat chance.)

E. If you must appear on the TV show *Cops*, at least wear a designer undershirt.

F. Police officers are acceptable in gay life only if they take it doggy style.

G. And that is all there is to be said about such people.

🐏 SPORTS

1. Body building is a gay sport that has as its purpose elevation of one's soul and the elevation of the blowjobs one receives in the sauna.

2. A gay gentleman may engage in lawn tennis and table tennis for his sporting life, since ice skating, gymnastics, and Roller Derby are clearly confined to more manly heterosexuals.

3. There are no lesbians in professional sports such as tennis, soccer, rugby, field hockey, volleyball, cycling, weightlifting, wrestling, running, jumping, or floor exercise. (Or at least *one* of these.)

4. Lipstick lesbians must not be put off by the shot put and try their very best.

5. Gay male rugby teams – and they do exist – are noted for their man-to-man contact and their impeccable hard-ons.

6. Baseball, football, soccer, and ice hockey teams are known for their institutionalized homophobia. Thus when said members stick it in each other they are just good, straight "buds" with short memories.

7. Sports teach boys healthy competition, as in breaking the opponent's will, to say nothing of fingers and noses. But the most important lesson is defining oneself as NOT A FAG.

8. It is difficult to show that gays and lesbians are STRONG when it comes to athletics, as long as their physical prowess is not matched by the moral courage to be "out."

9. Rowing is sort of like a circle jerk, except that the seating arrangement is different.

10. Try though you may, Tiddly Winks will not be an Olympic sport in the foreseeable future.

11. You can make a name for yourself in athletics, when gay, by winning the Tour de France or collecting autographed jock straps in locker rooms.

THE SPORTING LIFE

1. Being a good sport does not mean letting the f***ers keep you out of any sport you damn well want to play.

2. Straight men hate it, absolutely hate it, when defeated by any fag in any sport you care to name, so don't rub their faces in it. (Depending on what "it" is.)

3. (How does one put this judiciously?) Jock straps are never re-used after being come in.

4. Suck not off a referee during a time-out in any sport, lest it appear that you are taking unfair advantage of your heterosexual opponents, who will resent the referee's favoritism thereafter.

5. The Nineteenth Hole . . . means you really should cut down on the Cialis.

6. "Sweat" is a concept best left behind in the shower room, or dwelt upon in tranquility via celluloid representations, and not flung at the Duchess of Kent as you raise your trophy at Wimbledon.

7. The Gay Olympics demonstrate that gay men can be as obsessed with "balls" on the playing field as off.

8. The International Olympic Committee restrained the Gay Games from using the term Gay Olympics but let the Special Olympics use it. So it is obviously preferable to be retarded than gay. ('Retarded' is out as a term? Pish.)

9. Gladiatorial combats are still frowned upon in the finest circles, but you may watch World Federation Wrestling or Pride Fighting if your personal testosterone level is on empty. (Or you love camp.)

10. It is not true that jocks are stupid. Rather, they are inarticulately in awe of your verbal dexterity.

11. Intemperate or crude remarks about an opponent's wobbly buttocks are best replaced with "Good show!" or "Blimey!"

12. One may strengthen the grip in one's tennis hand by regular application of short, stiff strokes early in the morning or late at night, as long as you are alone, or with others.

13. Dancing can be a sport! Yes, it can. And you can tell someone is gay by the dancing style he prefers. Guess which
    a) the minuet, *b)* disco, *c)* square, *d)* dirty

Answer: all

FURTHER TRAVEL

1. Your own company may be the best company, if you are a leper, have any of the STD's, or are a Hindu fundamentalist.

2. When you set out on a long journey, unlike the ancient Egyptians, take your brains with you.

3. Bottled water has been proven to be at least as polluted as the waters at Lourdes. So don't be so self-righteous about your use of either.

4. Make yourself at home wherever you go, but don't pee in the pool at the Paris Hilton, unless you *are* Paris Hilton.

5. A train in Bosnia can be like a day in Kosovo!!

6. Club Med in East Berlin is said to be Six Stars in government travel brochures.

7. Head coverings for women in outlying Taliban areas are considered preferable, or milady may opt for seventy lashes instead.

8. There is no greater love than to forewarn another of a coming typhoon, or the absent of toilet paper in the bathroom.

9. Do not take your Louis Vuitton luggage with you as you prepare for your suicide bombing.

10. The Club Meds in Hawaii tend to be better for sunbathing than those in Minsk.

11. Hump not your tour guide's camel without the express, written consent of the local ayatollah.

12. A la Turk is the charming name for a hole to defecate in, common in certain un-modern regions, not to be confused in any way with Turkish Delight.

13. Stop cruising night and day, at least during the tsunami.

 # TREATMENT OF ANIMALS

Animal liberationists have a perfect right to object to the mistreatment of animals in far too many cultures. Brutal customs are not sanctioned simply because they have been around for centuries, or there would be no Animal or Gay Liberation Movements whatsoever.

1. Treat you gay pets as you would any others. But don't let them *marry* or it will upset the Great Chain of Being.

2. Guests may bring pets to some hotels, but, as Siegfried and Roy have taught us, tigers are not entirely suitable in supper clubs.

3. White toy poodles are out of fashion as the dog of choice. Mastiffs on steroids are in.

4. Do not give your cats "cute" names, as this is a clear sign that you have become your Great Aunt Thelma.

5. A designer collar for your cat or dog is fine. One for your goldfish is pretentious.

6. The British bring dogs into the dining room. And so do some Koreans. (Do not get confused

about the purpose of either if you ever hope to see Poopsie again.)

7. You are not allowed to French kiss your French poodle in public or private. (Unless you are a poodle yourself, or French, and then only on both cheeks.)

AH, THE THEATRE

1. One may not attend the theatre in one's undergarments. That sort of thing left to the performers.

2. Theatre is a battle between the buttocks and the brain. Increasingly, only the former triumph.

3. You may speak to the person next to you at the theatre when the person is suitable to your taste, if you are requesting more leg room or fancy a feel-up during the interval.

4. Leaving your gum under the seat is hardly the stuff of royalty.

5. Do not recite the lines of a play aloud along with the actors, however much you believe you excelled at school.

6. For every Jean Valjean hero there are twenty Inspector Javerts!

7. You needn't act like a half-wit merely because you got your ticker at the half-price booth.

8. If you remark, "I didn't know it was a musical!" in the twentieth year of the run of *Les Miserables*, maybe you are stupid.

9. You must pretend to enjoy a Harold Pinter play, whatever your true feelings.

10. For inner peace, choose a life in the theatre if you are an audience member, not an actor.

11. We understand that it is allowable nowadays for actors to be buried in sacred ground in marked graves.

12. Critics are to be obeyed without question, especially when they disagree.

13. *The New York Times* is just one man's opinion, just as Josef Stalin's was.

14. If you must cough, at least die by the end of the third act.

15. If you wrote the implausibilities of *Measure for Measure*, you would be drawn and quartered. You haven't been safely dead for four hundred years.

16. Color-blind casting is like foot-binding, in-explicable except as a cultural fetish.

17. Without homosexuals in the theatre, there would be no British actors – and no American audience.

🪶 FRESH CLICHÉS

A. Every dog will have his dog.

B. Prick up your ears? All right. Do what you must, but leave *our* ears alone.

C. Handsome is as handsome does. But the real question is: will handsome do me?

D. If you lend your sexual parts to a buyer for from twenty minutes to an hour, you are a whore. If you lend everything else but, you are a star.

E. British men perhaps exceed British women in looks by a smidgen. Possibly that is because your guide is a homosexual.

F. Cutting edge cuts both ways, for you if you're a minute too soon; against you if you're a minute too late. (See *Project Runway* from week to week.)

G. Derision of cleaning staff is beneath the finer sort, though a sharp glance at malingerers is in order.

H. It is not evil to demonize a demon.

I. The salt of the Earth often needs some pepper.

J. If you have to tell people you're famous, you're not.

THE EX-GAY MOVEMENT

One cannot fail to notice a movement underway in today's neo-conservative environment. While tradition in manners is all to the good, and can only be defended as right and proper, changing gays into straights may not be all it is cracked up to be. It is even rumored that it doesn't work. Just in case there are any doubts, here is

HOW TO TELL IF YOU ARE EX-GAY

1. You have pressed your genitalia among the pages of your Gideon.

2. You enjoy saving sex in the same position with the same woman for forty-eight and a half years.

3. You haven't had a thought, to say nothing of an orgasm, of your own ever since.

4. When you say your minister is "hot," you mean from delivering a fiery sermon about brimstone.

5. When you have sinful, lust-filled thoughts of sex with other men, you distract yourself by jacking off to Amy Grant videos.

6. You wish Oral Roberts would change his name,

7. You donate to Fred Phelps of Kansas to further 'The God Hates Fags' cause.

8. You can't wait for All You Can Eat Spaghetti Night at Carrow's.

9. You have saved your soul, but your soul is numb.

10. You Praise Jesus when you come in some hustler's mouth.

MORE TOASTS

1. "To real estate speculators trying to up their ill-gotten profits! . . . Up yours!"

2. "To steroid users: . . . Up mine!"

3. "To well-hung men! . . . The largest meal is not necessarily the tastiest!"

4. "To dumb presidents! . . . May history forget you, like you forgot it!"

5. "To those who con waitresses by pretending to order and then shooting up in the toilet before leaving! . . . May you shoot up with an empty syringe! "

6. "To the needy who try too hard, like comedian Chris Farley! . . . I wish you something I know you won't have: long life!"

7. "May you drink everyone else under the table! . . . Why people being under the table is important to you only you can say! "

8. "To basketball fans! . . . For God's sake, how many times can you watch a ball go through a hoop?!"

9. "Don't stop being needy (and creative) just because 17 states and the District of Columbia now say that you can pay alimony!"

10. "Politically correct is not always really correct!"

11. Remember, a toast is like a curse, only to people you sort of like!

You have been instructed

in all the subtleties of propriety.

Now go forth and Act Right!

This is the Third Edition of this book. Some 'interesting' changes have occurred over the years from 1982 to the present. In some places it is the best of times to be gay. In other places it is the worst. If you have chosen to be gay – and why wouldn't you? – remember to 1) be proud, but watch your back at all times, and 2) to be good, except when you shouldn't.

 # INDEX

Pages

TAKING THE BATHS
GLORY HOLES
INVITATIONS AND THANK-YOU NOTES
CONCENTRATION CAMPS
CHOOSING THE PROPER MATE
COMING-OUT PARTIES
BEING WELL-INFORMED
PROPER SPEECH
MAKE-UP / PLASTIC SURGERY
CORRESPONDENCE
SPORTS; PART TWO
ASTROLOGICAL SIGNS
GIFTS
KINKY SEX AND AMUSEMENT
HOW TO TELL – AH, ROMANCE
SAMPLE GREETING CARDS TO SEND
YACHTING
THE HELP
HEALTH; PART TWO
CORRESPONDENCE; PART TWO
BEING WELL-INFORMED; PART TWO
SMOKING
TRAVEL TIPS
PROPER SPEECH; PART THREE
COURTESY
ADDRESSING ROYALITY
SEX
BAR TIPS
CHANGING CUSTOMS
FOOD

MORE AIRPLANES
DORM LIFE
ILLEGAL AND DANGEROUS ACTIVITIES
PROPER DRAG
POLICE
SPORTS
THE SPORTING LIFE
FURTHER TRAVEL
TREATMENT OF ANIMALS
AH, THE THEATRE
FRESH CLICHÉS
THE EX-GAY MOVEMENT
MORE TOASTS